PIXIE DUST

PIXIE DUST

AND THE MEANING OF LIFE

GONCA ALBAN

Matador
9 Priory Business Park,
Wistow Road, Kibworth Beauchamp,
Leicestershire. LE8 0RX
Tel: 0116 279 2299
Email: books@troubador.co.uk
Web: www.troubador.co.uk/matador
Twitter: @matadorbooks

ISBN 978 1838593 445

British Library Cataloguing in Publication Data.
A catalogue record for this book is available from the British Library.

Printed and bound in the UK by TJ International, Padstow, Cornwall
Typeset in 11pt Aldine401 BT by Troubador Publishing Ltd, Leicester, UK

Matador is an imprint of Troubador Publishing Ltd

To Paul & Suzee Grilley

We create our world with our thoughts. First comes the thought, then the tangible reality. Remember this and take heart when you dream, hope and plan. But also remember it when you fear, worry or hate. Your world is what you make it.

"All that you are is the result of what you have thought." Sri Swami Sivananda

She woke up with a start. It was still dark and quiet. Her arm felt cold, the freezing winter night air breathing heavily on her arm, hands and face. She withdrew them quickly, snuggling her entire little body, her whole existence, underneath her warm duvet. She felt safe and comforted by its soft touch and huge size wrapped around her. The night air could thrash around as much as it wanted to, protected as she was at that moment, nothing could affect her sense of safety and comfort.

When suddenly an unexpected thing happened. She was sure she heard soft, gentle music, like bells ringing and laughter, maybe harps playing. Her curiosity aroused, she pricked up her ears and held her breath, focusing on the soft music. It was strange, so very unusual, nothing like any music she had ever heard before. The sound was soft, yet it surrounded her whole little world, all else muted by it. It felt like a smooth, soft fog had descended down from heaven.

As she lifted a side of her duvet up, just enough to get a glimpse of her surroundings, she was stunned by a pure light, golden yellow, yet soft like the music. Rather than being dazzling, it was bright without hurting her eyes.

Mesmerised, she lifted a little more of the duvet off herself, then a little more. She could not tell where the music was coming from, but then, she was too lost in the vision of the moment to remember what had first driven her to take a peak.

1

The light was spread evenly throughout her room. She could find no source or focal point to it. She noticed the bits of fabric she had collected and hung around her walls (she thought it was rather artistic and imaginative of her) were floating and dancing, still attached to the wall, but lifting and moving in wave like motions away from it, as if blown by a caressing gentle breeze, a breeze that would have needed to come out of the wall to float them in that way. Their colours had been transformed, along with everything else in the room. They looked so much warmer and more vibrant than they had done when she went to bed. She reached out to them wanting to connect to their softness and warm glow. And it was exactly at that moment that she saw her, the source of the enchanting music. Only she was not playing anything, nor was she singing, nor was her mouth moving. Only her eyes. They were bright, glittering, smiling, shining. They twinkled and danced. Mira felt like she'd just come across the very source of joy and excitement. There was warmth in her smile and it was her eyes that were doing the smiling.

Mira smiled back. It would have been impossible not to. Her joy was contagious. She felt like her heart was taking on the same glow as her room. In her excitement she'd forgotten about sleep and where she was and what an extraordinary sight this was. It all felt rather natural now, as if she had been expecting this all along. Her still uplifted hand changed course and reached towards this shining being, her fairy, angel and star. Her new friend.

"What are you?" she found herself whispering. Or at least she thought she had said it out loud, but within a moment of her uttering the words she was no longer sure. It was practically as if the warm glow of the room had enveloped her words and muffled them into nothingness. But her new friend answered, without moving her lips. Mira was surprised to find that she had heard what the magical being said.

"Pixie. And this golden glow, the light, the warmth, that's all pixie dust. It's magic Mira. Do you believe in magic?

"I used to, but I don't anymore. I grew up" she replied, puffing up slightly in a self-important way. She was of course above these things now.

But after a moment's thought she added, "but you seem like magic to me. Are you a fairy?"

"I'm whatever you want me to be. Well, within limits. I can make wishes come true if they are going to help you, but only temporarily. You can make a wish, enjoy it for a while, and then you have to return back to where you were. Do you think that's magic Mira?"

"That doesn't sound like much of a gift" Mira said , but very quickly added apologetically "I mean if they're only temporary that is."

"Oh but it is a gift. You see, the wish might be temporary, but your experience, what you learn, the pleasure, the things you see and people you meet, the fun you have, the memories, whatever you fill your wish time with, those all remain with you, forever. You can use what you experience and learn for the rest of your life, in any way you want."

Mira looked around her with a sceptical expression on her face, her brow creased slightly as she tried to understand what Pixie had been saying. All she had understood from all of this was that she could make a wish, it would come true, but only for a short time.

"For how long?"

Mira's question disrupted Pixie's flow and for a moment she had no idea what Mira was referring to.

"For how long will my wish be true?"

"Hmm. I'd never thought of that. For as long as necessary I suppose. You see, it's simple really. You have a reason to want something. It could be because you've never experienced it and you've heard about it somewhere and you want to have, do or see it too. Well then, you'll have it until you are satisfied. Or maybe you need to learn something and you're driven to ask for something." Now she was faltering, thinking hard, trying to find words, slowing down. "And well, then, you'll have the experience until you've learned what it is you need to learn."

"But then what if I never have enough? Then it would be a an everlasting wish?"

"Well, yes, in theory, if you never had enough, you would carry on forever and ever." Pixie looked puzzled, she was thinking hard. No, she was sure that had never happened.

"But you see, you're human. You will have enough or get bored, or want more or better or different… And each pleasurable experience comes with its downside. There's no pleasure without its shadow and vice versa. But anyway, that's a lesson for another time… "

"So, tell me what you would like to wish for", she added after a short pause.

Mira's mind went blank. Completely blank. There were so many things she always wished she could do or see and yet at that moment she might as well of never had a single wish in her life. Now she was placed on the spot, there really was nothing she could think of. And yet, she knew there was so much… In fact, everything. If she had limitless wishes she would change everything in her life and everything about her life, be anywhere else, with anyone else, doing whatever else, it practically didn't matter exactly what. As long as she could get away. Wasn't that in essence what she had always wanted?

So within a few minutes she went from not being able to think of a single wish, to having way too many to be able to choose one. Her mind went from a complete blank to an airport terminal. It was too busy, too loud, too fast. And she was no closer to saying anything. She simply looked up with wide eyes at Pixie, who was still smiling and shining. Was everything in life always so full of excitement for her?

But Pixie understood. After a few moments, she said "tell you what, whatever you choose or do right now, you won't be able to engage in it or enjoy it. You look like a stunned rabbit. I'll be back tomorrow night, and in the meantime you can think about what you'd like to have first"

"No, no", Mira was stirred into action very quickly by these words. She didn't want Pixie to leave. What if she didn't come back? She didn't want her to leave yet, maybe not ever. Her glow and music were so peaceful like a supportive wrap snuggling in all around her. She needed a friend. She needed a moment, she needed some time. "My wish is that you don't leave me"

"Ever" she added after a pause.

Pixie smiled with a little sadness in her eyes now. "Sweetie, I told you, nothing I grant will last forever, even if you wish it"

And then, practically as an afterthought "But what you learn, what you make out of the gifts, whether through watching, listening, seeing, or experiencing, or whether through effort, tears and pain, or laughter, whatever you yourself make of your wishes that are granted, well those will stay with you, for as long as you live. So make the most of every single wish, whether the outcome is fun or not, whether it hurts or fulfils, whether there's disappointment or joy, take what you can from each and every one. Enjoy the fun, laugh with the funny, cry with the sad, learn from the wise, in fact learn from it all." She stopped. She could see her words were having no effect on Mira whatsoever.

"I'll be back tomorrow, I promise"

And with a last smile and flash of light she was gone and so was the warmth and the light. The floating fabrics were no longer dancing. Stillness prevailed. Stillness in the room and stillness within. Mira was too stunned to move or think. Her mind lingered on Pixie's last words. "She said she will come back tomorrow night. So she will" she told herself, several times, willing her heart to believe the words that had been uttered.

The room felt cold and dark in Pixie's absence. It felt like such a lonely, little place after her short-lived vision. Mira buried herself back between sheets and under her duvet, searching for some warmth and comfort, but she could find none. The feeling she received from them paled in contrast to what she had just experienced. She felt more alone at that moment than she had ever felt before, her world seemed so much darker and colder.

She panicked as she noticed that the memory was already fading away from her. She could no longer be sure if it had really happened or not. Pixie's face was becoming vague and hazy. The tune was lost in the night. The golden warm colour had been swallowed by darkness.

She fell asleep, her face wet with tears, hugging her toy tiger, curled into a ball, cold in spite of the warm room and duvet.

The next morning, as soon as the sun had poked its misty head above the horizon, Mira woke up excited, although at first she could not remember why. The first thing she noticed was a flutter in her heart. She bolted upright in bed, her eyes wide open. For a moment she held her breath, forcing stillness over her body and mind. She remained quiet, listening, for what she wasn't sure, but definitely with a sense of expectation.

Then she slowly drew her covers away from her and gingerly stepped out onto the cold stone floor, very quietly and carefully, as if she was afraid to startle someone or something. Her mind continued in its expectant, blank state at first. It had not yet started to fully function. She was still experiencing the empty gap after waking and before the first thoughts start flow in.

It was a cold, cloudy day. The mist sat heavy and looked settled in the skies, clouds weighing their burdened moisture down on the world. The whole sky was a burden, a heavy weight pressing down on earth.

Then, gradually, thoughts started to stream back in. She remembered Pixie and their encounter the night before. She was half hoping to see her little angel, but there was no sight of her. She felt a little confused. Could it have all been a dream? Her heart fell. Only a magical dream after all. Perhaps. And yet, it felt so real. And unreal at the same time.

Disappointment took over her as she made her way in to the bathroom. She was trying to bring up all she had seen and every word Pixie had said as she washed her face. She paused and closed her eyes tightly, bringing back to her mind Pixie's face and shining light, her brightness and smell.

Gradually the whole conversation started coming back to her. And with a jerk she stopped her movements half way through brushing her teeth. "It was real" she thought. "It wasn't a dream. Pixie was here. She told me I could wish for anything and that she would return today" Her excitement clambered back and spread. She tried to hold it in. She hated feeling disappointed. She hesitated even within her growing hope and excitement. A part of her was afraid to believe and trust too much. What if it was a dream? But then another, greater part of her felt sure.

She went back to her room and started getting dressed. She picked out her clothes carefully, wanting to be prepared when Pixie returned, if she returned…

"Oh Pixie, please come back" she thought.

Mira struggled to get through her day. It was one of those usual, run of the mill days and her mind was overloaded with thoughts of Pixie. She could not concentrate on or enjoy anything. Her entire being was focused on the meeting with Pixie she hoped beyond hope would take place that night. Her breakfast went down unnoticed. The skies cleared, yet Mira was still cloudy with thoughts and questions.

About half way through the day a thought occurred to her. "Well, just in case" she thought "I should be prepared. What would I wish for if Pixie returned tonight?" But once more she could think of nothing at all. And then, just as had happened the night before, she thought of way too many things, none of them convincing her little heart. None of them stuck out as the obvious number one. They were all exciting possibilities, but which to pick? Should she wish to go away? But where? She could wish to live in a palace and be served all day and night perhaps. Or she could wish to fly. Maybe she could wish for a dog?

None of these wishes felt overwhelmingly right, none clicked. None of them were things she wanted with her whole heart and soul, they were parts of a whole, but not the whole. But what did she want then? What was the big picture she was trying to put together with her little wishes?

She went out into the garden, walking amongst the bare trees. They had shed their leaves months ago. There was frost on the shrubs and the frosted earth crunched under her feet.

A lone chirping bird caught her eye. "What shall I wish for little bird? I can't think of anything" Tears were welling up in her eyes, pushed up to the surface by her exasperation.

"Blast this. Pixie's not coming back anyway. Who's heard of such a thing. Any wish indeed. It was just a dream" And with that she gave up and crunched her way back to her room. Her mind was grinding to a halt, tired out by all the thinking, struggling, questioning and puzzling.

"I wish I could know what I want" she cried. And with that she felt the whole room shake. A warm golden light started to glow, lightly at first, but gradually increasing in strength. As if the sun was rising on a warm, clear day. The light had no source, none that she could see, even though she was prepared this time and looking out for it. Then she saw a full blast glow and sparkle in the corner and Pixie appeared before her eyes. She looked exactly like a fairy should look. Perhaps those who drew pictures of fairies in books had seen Pixie too. Once she appeared, it was as if she had never left at all. How funny that Mira had not been able to bring a clear picture of her into her mind before. She exuded life, sparkling and full of light. And that wonderful, playful shine twinkling in her eyes, out of her whole being.

"At last, you have found a wish"

"But that's not a wish" Mira cried panicking. "It's not a real wish. I don't want to use my wish on that. I want to know what to wish for and ask for that. That doesn't count"

"Oh why little girl. So wise, yet so naive. It's the best wish I've ever heard anyone ask for. If everyone knew what they truly wanted, then the world would be such a happy place. Instead people waste their whole lives running after things that don't make them happy. Chasing one dream after another, only to find none of them satisfy them or bring them happiness. Once you know what you truly want, then everything else falls into place. You see, you don't need me if you know what you want, you can have it without a wish fulfilling fairy. But never mind that for now, you'll see for yourself some day. For now, let's grant you your wish"

Mira waited, expecting the answer to her question to appear in her mind, but no inspiration or thought came.

"It didn't work" she said, still sulky.

Pixie laughed. "Honey, what in the world made you think you would have your wish with the click of a finger. You are going to need to find out, through experience. Don't worry sweetheart, you'll get what you want. Just play along with me and keep your eyes, mind and heart open. If you're all sulky like this, how can any inspiration come in? Living involves being open to everything and experiencing fully, not shutting down at every turn with disappointment"

Mira was not convinced, but Pixie's joy was contagious and she couldn't help becoming just a little bit curious, enough to lift her eyes up and feel some excitement creep into her heart, in spite of her strong efforts for it not to. She was trying her hardest to remain sulky and grown up.

She looked around, but everything was still the same. Pixie was still smiling at her. She was just about to open her mouth to ask more questions when Pixie said "That's better. Now close your eyes and don't open them again until I say so"

Mira took one last look at Pixie, feeling hope rise up in her once more. She couldn't help but feel excited. She shut her eyes tight. "Oh, take me away from here" she thought, "as far, far away as possible, somewhere new and very different" "and warm" she added as an afterthought.

"Open your eyes" Mira heard, but found that for a moment she simply could not. She was afraid of what she might see, of her wish coming true, as well as it not coming true and being disappointed. Slowly she forced her eyelids up and exclaimed with delight. "Oh Pixie, this is wonderful"

She was standing in the centre of a small opening, in the midst of a large, green forest, with bright, warm sunlight shining down on her skin. She lifted her face to the sun, enjoying the warmth and the light, then lowered her gaze again to take in her surroundings. The forest was full of lush and bright colours. Deep greens, reds and whites, yellows and blues, all shades of them. Mira felt alive, the vibrancy of the forest pulsating through the cells of her body, adding to her excited energy. She heard birds chirping happily and saw the tail of a rabbit vanish into the undergrowth.

"Oh Pixie, this is wonderful" she said again, "I never want to leave. It's heaven, Pixie". After a quick thought she added, "Is it heaven, Pixie? Is that where I am?"

"No honey, not quite, but it's your current heaven, the way you've imagined it to be"

"Can I go into the forest?"

"Of course, it's yours"

"Is it safe?"

"As safe as you imagine it to be, honey. Remember, you're creating the forest with your thoughts as you go along, so think of safe and nice things and that's what you'll get"

Mira was overjoyed. She ran in a random direction, and as she ran, the clearing moved with her, near enough for her to step back into it, if she wanted to. As dense as the forest had seemed from the outside, as she ran in, the sun still managed to reach her, branches opening up just enough to let its warm rays in, warming her heart as well as her skin. Many rabbits appeared, at first they ran away from her, but gradually they grew less timid and started to stop and draw closer instead, their dancing noses and curious eyes directed directly at her. Mira felt so happy, she thought she might burst with joy.

She touched the trunk of a tree and the tree looked down at her and smiled. "I'm okay in this forest" she thought, "All I feel around me is love. It will take care of me"

She saw a mango tree appear in front of her, its branches weighed down heavily with ripe fruit. She reached up and pulled one off. Just as she was wondering how she could possibly cut into it, a knife appeared at the base of the tree. She picked it up and looked around. She wanted to offer Pixie some, but Pixie had vanished. A moment's fear crept in, but she brushed it aside "it's okay, the forest is your friend, you're safe here". But she wanted to share her joy and laugh and talk with someone. She looked around again and there Pixie was, laughing at her. "I can keep you company for now" she said.

Mira spent hours exploring the forest, trying different fruits, stroking animals, climbing trees, thoroughly enjoying herself, her child mind and heart open to the wonders of everything around her. It was all going so well, when suddenly a thought occurred to her.

"So is this it then Pixie? Is this what I truly want?"

Pixie laughed again, she seemed to be always laughing "not quite honey. This is you figuring out what it is you truly want. Be patient. Enjoy what you have. Don't worry, all your questions will be answered in good time"

Mira hesitated, but not for long. What did it really matter. She was so happy at that moment, she no longer wanted anything else. "I think this is what I want Pixie. I think I'll stay here forever and ever and ever" And with that, off she went again, kicking up leaves, picking flowers and singing along the way.

After a while she started to feel tired, and even a little bored. "What else is there to do here Pixie?" she asked, not able to think of anything else she really truly wanted to do. How could she possibly top this experience, or make it better? She felt like she'd already had the best day of her life and the day wasn't even over yet. How was she going to fill the rest of her time?

"Pixie, I think I'm bored" she said, tears appearing in her eyes. She had never felt so happy and had so much fun and seen so much beauty. She didn't want to let go. She didn't want it to stop. She wanted to stay there always, but she couldn't think of anything to do.

"What do people do here Pixie? I want to stay, but I can't think of anything else to do"

Pixie replied, "it's your world Mira, you decide what you want to do"

Mira flopped down on some grass. "But I don't want to have to do anything. I want to be able to run around and have fun and have nothing to do"

"Well than, do that"

"But I'm bored"

"I can't help you decide Mira. I'm only here to make your wishes come true. I can't choose your wishes for you"

Mira decided to sleep, maybe ideas would come to her the next day. She was tired anyway. But then a terrible thought occurred to her.

"Will all this vanish if I go to sleep? Will I wake up in my old room again?"

"Only if you wish it to be so. Now stop worrying. Remember even if you find yourself back where you were, you can always wish to be here again"

Mira hesitated. She was afraid of not being able to return. "Maybe I'll stay awake then". But she'd had a full morning and eventually fatigue took over. She fell asleep in spite of her best efforts not to.

She woke up back in her own room the next morning. There was a denseness in her heart and at first she did not know why. Then gradually the events of the previous day came back to her. She lay still and quiet. "I wish Pixie was here with me" she thought and closed her eyes. Sure enough, she felt a warmth spread over her. She opened her eyes slowly, half fearing it was her imagination playing tricks on her. But there Pixie was, radiant as ever. "You came" she whispered, some of the denseness lifting away from her heart. Pixie simply smiled.

12

"How come you're always happy Pixie? You laugh all the time. How is that? Even when I'm happy, doubts and fears have a way of creeping in. I can't help it, they taint my joy."

"That's for you to find out Mira. But for now, try and enjoy every moment of every day, wherever you are and don't worry about the moment that is to follow. Each moment can be full of excitement and joy and if you live in each moment and exclusively in that moment, then you can always feel happy and excited. You're unhappy now only because you're worried about what might happen next, or tomorrow. Think about it, you wished for me and here I am. If there's anything else you wish for, that also will be yours. Whatever more can you want?"

"I want to go back to the magical forest"

"Well then, it's done. Close your eyes"

Mira obeyed and in a flash, there she was, back in the glow of warm sunlight, in her beautiful forest. She wanted more of it this time though. So she searched her brain for how she could make the forest and her experience even better, more fun and more beautiful.

"I wish to play with the animals" she thought, "I wish to understand them and speak to them"

She caught sight of a hedgehog moving along slowly only a few steps away from her. "Hi hedgehog", she called out. The hedgehog turned its little head and lifted its nose up at her, wrinkling its face in the process. "Oh hello there little girl. What an odd sight you are. We don't see human beings in this forest. And I'm sure I've never heard of one that can speak to us. I've certainly not met a human myself. In fact, as far as I know, they're usually too wrapped in themselves to notice us or pay attention to what we say, so we stopped even trying to talk to them a long time ago. My grandmother always says 'Keep away from them humans. They're not interested in our wellbeing and we're safer and better off without them'. How come you're speaking to me now?"

"I want to get to know you" she replied simply.

13

The hedgehog scratched its head. "There's not much to know really. I'll tell you what, why don't you come home with me for tea? There you can meet my whole family and find out what you want"

"I would love that" Mira replied, full of excitement once more. But then a puzzled expression spread over her face. "You drink tea?"

"We'll drink whatever you fancy. Come along then, follow me. Mind your step now, you don't want to step on those ants over there"

"There's a girl" the hedgehog remarked, pleased with himself and the result as Mira gingerly stepped to one side and very very carefully followed her new friend.

"Is it far?" she asked, more to fill the silence than anything else. She thought she could follow the hedgehog for days without caring when they arrived, she was too surprised to mind.

"No, no, not at all, nearly there"

They reached a tree with branches so full of leaves and hanging so low to the ground, it looked like someone had hung a tent over its trunk. Mira followed the hedgehog, scrambling on all fours through a little gap under some branches. When she was through, she was amazed at the scene that awaited her. There, under the branches, in an immaculately swept clearing sat a variety of small animals in a circle, evidently waiting for her, with a pot of tea and an assortment of cups stacked around it, all waiting to be filled.

Not all the animals gathered in this makeshift, natural tent were hedgehogs either. Other than her guide, there were two more hedgehogs. But there were also two rats, a rabbit, a lizard, a small group of mice, a squirrel and what looked like a bat too, hanging upside down from one of the branches.

Too amazed to say anything Mira sat down with a loud thud, joining the circle of animals. They were all smiling at her, waiting for her to speak first.

She turned towards her hedgehog guide, but he had joined the other two hedgehogs and she no longer knew which one he was. She decided to speak vaguely in that direction, looking at each one of them in turn "I didn't know you all got on with each other. With other kinds of animals I mean. I thought animals stuck with their own kind and fought with the others"

"Well, no, we're not always at each other's throats. Not all of us. If that's what you mean" replied one of them, but it was a gentle, female voice, so Mira knew that wasn't her guide. She continued "We gathered together because we thought this would be a nice way for you to make the acquaintance of some of our friends" With that she looked lovingly into the eyes of one of the other hedgehogs and then smiled again. They must be together, Mira thought, but how in the world will I recognise each one of them?

As if it had read her mind, the squirrel spoke up "don't worry, you'll get used to us and start to see the differences. We're like you, all humans look the same to us at first, though they smell different for sure" At this the little gang giggled and nodded and for a moment the place rang with joyful clamour.

"Oh" she said, then added, not wanting to sound silly or dumb, "yes".

The rabbit then took the lead and started arranging the cups, pouring tea into each one. Mira stared as she watched it keep pouring until all the cups were full, and yet the teapot couldn't have been large enough to fill more than two of those cups. Then the bat released its grip from the branch, flew over to the cups, picked one up in its beak and without spilling a drop flew over to Mira with it. Too stunned to move Mira stared at it. She heard squealing laughter from the group of mice and then the rat spoke up "well, take it. Poor bat is going to get tired if you keep him there for much longer. And anyway, he needs a free beak to pass the rest of the cups out to us".

Mira felt herself blush, she apologised, took the cup and thanked the bat, then watched him repeat the process until all the cups had been handed out, or beaked out rather. She watched as each animal took hold of its cup with little paws and started sipping daintily.

"Well?" said rat, "do you like it?"

Once more Mira felt colour rise up to her cheeks. She felt ashamed of herself and speedily picked the cup up and took a big gulp, only to spit it out again. "Oh, I'm so sorry" she cried, feeling increasingly exasperated, "it's so hot". She started mopping up the spilled tea with a corner of her dress.

"Oh don't you worry", the female hedgehog said kindly. "We've all done it. Take your time, it'll cool down". Her voice was so kind, Mira relaxed a little and copying the animals' movements took the cup back to her lips, blew on it and then took a tiny sip.

"Delicious!" she remarked as her first sip lingered in her mouth and eased down her throat. "the best I've ever had" she added. This comment seemed to please them all immensely and they threw satisfied glances at each other before turning their gaze back on her.

She continued to sip and watch as the gathering of animals chattered between themselves when suddenly a thought occurred to her.

"I thought bats ate mice" she remarked, a little too suddenly, breaking into the pleasant atmosphere. She had just remembered her biology lesson. They all stopped speaking at once and stared at her, perplexed and bemused. Mira felt embarrassed. "I mean, I thought they didn't get along. That's what I was taught." "At school", she added, as if that would make things better and explain her ignorance away.

The gentle hedgehog was the first one to speak up again, always coming to her rescue. Such a sensitive, kind animal, thought Mira.

"Not here honey. Here all animals get along"

Then she glanced at Mira with questioning eyes "at least I think they do. Isn't that the way you wish it to be?"

And with a flash Mira understood. Her wish had not only brought her into the perfect forest, where animals were friendly and invited her over to tea, but she had also wished them to be nice and peaceful. A fear shot through her. So much power. What if she wished for something bad? Like the bat suddenly turning on a mouse and whisking it away to eat it. How unbearable that would be. And quick as a flash, before Mira had even taken in her own thought, the bat had shot up, grabbed a mouse and flew off with the poor little mouse screaming for help as it lay petrified and trapped in its clamped mouth.

"Oh no", cried Mira, "what have I done? I did not wish that. In fact I was just thinking how terrible it would be if I wished it. Oh, what can I do? I've ruined it all." She was full of fear and embarrassment. A sense of hopelessness took over her. She felt stunned and all she could do was wish to vanish, to be back in her home, safe where she could not harm anyone.

And once again, her wish came true the next instant. She found herself staring at her wall, seated uncomfortably on her old bed. "Oh no" she thought again and started to cry. She felt forlorn and heartbroken. How much worse this was. All that beautiful experience ruined. She had killed a friendly mouse. How could she take it back?

"I wish I could control my thoughts. I wish I wasn't alive. I wish I hadn't hurt that poor mouse" She was sobbing loudly when she felt the familiar warmth of Pixie's presence.

"Oh Pixie, what have I done? I don't deserve your gift. I killed the poor mouse"

"What nonsense" Pixie replied, although she wasn't laughing this time. "How could you have killed something that was only there as a figment of your imagination in the first place?

"So it wasn't real? None of this is real? It's all just a dream?" Mira's eyes opened wide. She had forgotten all about her pain and tears.

"Well, only as real as anything else around you."

This confused Mira, but she kept quiet.

"Now dry your eyes and rest. Everything will seem much better once you wake up." With that Pixie helped Mira lie in her bed, carefully tucking in the sides of the duvet. Then she gave her a gentle warm kiss on her forehead and was gone. She had vanished so quickly, Mira had not had a chance to gather her thoughts or to cry out or ask anything else. And very quickly she was fast asleep, as if Pixie's kiss had cast a magic spell on her.

"Once when I was meditating I heard His voice, whispering: "Thou dost say I am away, but thou didst not come in. That is why thou dost say I am away. I am always in. Come in and thou wilt see Me. I am always here, ready to greet thee." Paramahansa Yogananda, Man's Eternal Quest (revealing God's message to him)

Mira woke up feeling refreshed and in much better spirits than she had been feeling at the end of the previous day, but as the day progressed, her mood deteriorated. There was no sign of Pixie anywhere. Several times she thought of wishing Pixie to appear by her side to help her through her mood and sadness, but each time, she pushed the thought away, feeling too ashamed and afraid. She had been given a wish, which had placed her in a position of power over beautiful living beings and she had misused her power, although unwillingly, killing a gentle, talking mouse as a result. Who knows what other disasters her uncontrolled thoughts might cause. She was evil at the core and that was obvious. Her parents were right after all. She could not be entrusted with such a precious gift. She neither deserved it, nor was she the right person to hold it.

She made it through the day feeling grey and unhappy. All day the only thing she could think of wanting was to be back under her covers in safety. And as it always does in no matter what circumstances, time did eventually pass, although far more slowly than it usually did. After what felt to her like an entire lifetime, eventually, she got in to bed. For her it was the end of a terrible and distressing day and she could not wait for it to be over and done with.

Many days passed in this way. Mira could never quite find in herself enough courage to wish for Pixie. She kept putting off another encounter. Days turned into weeks and weeks into years. Her memories slowly faded. Gradually her life took over and with time she forgot the whole incident.

Mira grew up into a beautiful young woman. Those who knew her would have said that she was spirited, had great inner strength and a mind of her own. She had a kind heart. And yet, inside her, she was always aware of a growing sense of unease. She was never able to feel quite settled and content. Something seemed to be missing in her life, or as she thought of it, in her soul. No matter what she achieved, whatever she did, there was always a sense of not quite enough, not good enough, nor quite right. She tended to assume it was her lack and maybe she just did not know how to be fully happy. Perhaps she was simply born that way, defective in some fundamental way. Times in her life when she experienced full happiness seemed to pass all too soon, leaving their place to that well-known sense of loss. Sometimes she thought happiness was within her grasp, if only she knew how to reach out to it. Or perhaps it was already there, hers for the taking, if only she could change herself so that she could deserve it. After all, wasn't it all her fault? If she felt a sense of lack, that was her inability to feel happy, not due to her circumstances or surroundings. Everyone else seemed happy with their lot, making the most of whatever they had in front of them. It bemused her to see laughter and joy, people with untiring energy and enthusiasm, rushing around as if any of this mattered. And in some way she felt separate from it all, different from others.

At times it all seemed so irrelevant to her; both the sorrows and the joys. And at times she hated herself for not caring more. And other times she berated herself for caring too much. She could never get it right.

She moved away from home the first chance she got and started a new life in the city. As noisy, busy and polluted as the city was, it was where her work and friends were, the place she called home. She loved her work and found great joy and satisfaction in it. Her life was good, she knew that and was grateful for it. She lacked nothing that was obvious. And yet still, somewhere in the background, when she was still enough, for long enough, was still that familiar sense of something missing.

Mira had some time off work and it was a dull, grey day. The skies seemed to want to burst into heavy rain, yet something kept them together, blocked and dense. They clung on to the heavy water, weighing down on earth. Mira felt they were burdening her soul also; closing down on her chest, the air inside too dense to breathe and a dense blanket of gloom lay thick outside. She made her coffee and truly relished her first cup, as she always did. She was gazing mindlessly out of the window wondering how she could make use of her time off. The weather was too gloomy to be inviting and she had little desire to go out. She couldn't be bothered to go to a museum and she didn't particularly want to meet anyone either. She had promised herself that this week of no work would be her gift to herself, a time with no plans, no commitments, simply time off, a blank sheet, anything goes…

On a whim she decided to clear out some of her old stuff. A bit of cleaning would brighten the place, and then maybe she could write. She started pulling out boxes in a bustle of all efficiency. But as soon as they were open, they seemed too full, the mountain of stuff in them insurmountable and way too irrelevant and uninteresting. So she kept moving on from one box to the next, accomplishing nothing and her mood darkening and listlessness growing with each box she opened. She couldn't be bothered to sort anything out. Cleaning had been a bad idea.

Just as she was about to give up and pile the boxes back into their storage space, she came across a neatly bound notebook. It had a dried flower carefully taped onto its cover. It looked pretty and dainty. Mira opened it. It was her diary from when she was a child. Only a few pages had been written into, and then obviously the diary had been abandoned, but put aside and kept carefully nonetheless.

Mira thought this was odd. She had kept a diary since the age of six and she had boxes of notebooks full of them. Why would she have left aside this pretty little notebook, tucked it away separate from the others and started a new one when it had been barely used?

Curiosity moved her hands and she opened up to the first page and started reading. As she read, vague memories started stirring in her. She read about Pixie. "I must have wanted a separate, special diary to record my experiences with Pixie", she thought. She read to the end, where she had stated in capital letters: I AM TOO BAD TO BE GIVEN SUCH A PRECIOUS GIFT. NEVER AGAIN WILL I WISH FOR ANYTHING! She had signed it too. And with that the diary had been shut for good.

Mira closed her eyes, trying to remember all the details of her experience. Was it even real? It had only been a couple of nights after all. Maybe it had only been a dream, a creation of her mind resulting from her wanting to go away and be in some magical land elsewhere instead of where she had been, feeling tormented at her parents' home. She did have a vivid imagination after all.

She got up and made herself some more coffee, musing over what she had read. Why not, she thought. Why couldn't it be true?

She started wondering what she would wish for now. It struck her as fascinating that in spite of more than twenty years passing by, her essential wish had not changed that much. She wanted to know what to wish for, what would truly make her happy, deeply, in a lasting way. No matter how wonderful her life was at times, did she not always have the feeling that something was missing? If she knew what was missing, she could get it herself, then she wouldn't need an angel of magic. But first she needed to know what she needed, what to aim for.

"How funny", she thought," as a six year old I was certainly smarter than I've ever given myself credit for". Then, half in jest and with barely any hope "I wish Pixie to enter my life again" she said out loud, but there was no conviction in her words. She didn't believe Pixie would appear anyway, and of course Pixie didn't.

Throughout the day, no matter what Mira did, she could not shake the thoughts of Pixie and the memories out of her mind. "But this IS what I want" she cried out, feeling exasperated at one point. "I want to discover what the best way to live my life is and I need help with that. It doesn't have to come in the form of a wish-fulfilling angel, but I need guidance and help in whatever way or shape it does come"

And with those heartfelt cries she felt a gentle rumbling and a warm golden light appeared and started to spread in an even, smooth way. To Mira's utter amazement there she was, Pixie, just as she had described her in her little diary, sparkling, shining, smiling.

"Ah, so at last you remembered me" said Pixie laughing. "I could have given up on you, you know. It's been so long. As children you humans tend to believe anything is possible, that you can do and achieve anything, wish for anything and that life will bring you joy. When young, you're still connected to angels, fairies, stars. But then as you grow up, you forget... You start to become dull, losing your connection to your inner magic. Knocked about by life, you lose faith. Oh, I'm so glad you've found me again, Mira"

"How? What? Wow!" were the first shocked and meaningless words that came out of Mira's mouth. She was too stunned to speak for a few minutes and Pixie let her take her time.

"So I can wish for anything I want?"

"Yes"

"Can I wish for something like, I don't know, how to live a meaningful life? How to be always every moment happy? Can I wish that all humans feel nothing but love and compassion for each other? World peace maybe? Can I wish to restore the world's forests?" Mira's head was buzzing. She was reeling off whatever came to her mind.

"Well" Pixie said slowly, "I suppose you could. But I wonder if you would if you understood more"

Then she sparkled up again. "I have an idea. You did wish for guidance and help after all and that was the most heartfelt wish I have ever heard, so that's what I will give you. I think you need to learn and see some things before being given the power to change the world in such fundamental ways. You see, down on earth, without wisdom and understanding of the way everything works, you tend to misunderstand… And in fact that's the cause of all unhappiness in the first place. In fact, the more you understand, the happier and more content you'll be and you'll realise everything has a reason and value, even suffering. You'll likely find the best way to live your life too. So all in one. Sound like a good plan?"

"Okay. Yes. Guide me, show me whatever you see fit. Just don't let me make any stupid or harmful wishes please"

"It's always going to be your decision what you wish for Mira, that's the way it is. But I'll tell you what. I promise to always warn you before you make such a wish and then it will still be up to you"

"That's fine with me. I can't imagine deciding against what you advise"

Pixie smiled at this. "Don't you humans quite often go against what you know is right, or what someone wiser has advised you? You even ignore your own instincts and intuition more often than not. Until you forget their existence. Never mind for now, you will see."

There was a pause. Mira was waiting for something to happen, but nothing did.

"So what now?" she asked.

"Nothing more today. I'll leave you for now and let our meeting settle in. I want to give you some time to think. Also, I need some time to think where to take you first. After that it will be easy. Each experience you have will guide me and you towards what you need next. So rest, dear Mira. I'll be back tomorrow"

And with a flash she was gone. The room felt unbearably desolate suddenly. The cold grey air was pushing its weight even more forcefully now and the contrast between Pixie's warm, glowing light and the grey and cold of Mira's real world felt unbearably jarring. Mira sat in the exact same spot Pixie had left her without moving for a very long time. She was too stunned, excited and nervous to even dare take big breaths. Eventually she decided to get ready for bed. Early though it still was, she wanted to be fresh for her adventure of the next day and she could think of absolutely nothing else worth doing. Once asleep, she would no longer feel anxious or count each second as it passed by. It was her way out.

"You have the power to hurt yourself or to benefit yourself…
If you do not choose to be happy no one can make you happy.
Do not blame God for that! And if you choose to be happy, no
one can make you unhappy… It is we who make of life what
it is." Paramahansa Yogananda, Spiritual Diary

"… happiness is determined more by one's state of mind than
by external events" HH Dalai Lama, The Art of Happiness

"Happiness is a how, not a what, a talent, nor an object"
Hermann Hesse

Mira woke up feeling excited for the first time in a long while. Today would be the start of a new adventure. One that would, if Pixie held true to her word, give her un understanding of what to do with her life, how to live it and how to be happy all the time.

She was glad she had made the wish she had. She trusted Pixie and knew in her heart she would need to be guided in the right direction. How often in her life she had been struck by how vague the boundary between good and bad, right and wrong was. She had decided that there was no such thing as pure good or right. Wasn't it after all about what you do with the results of your decisions, that makes your life what it is? What is 'good' any way? Does it not after all always come with a bit of what is 'bad' and is not the opposite also true? So often our decisions come with unexpected outcomes. How often she had struggled to make decisions, not sure which would be the right course to take. So much of life was shades of grey, good from one angle and could be bad from another. And again, what is good? What is bad? Even the worst criminal has a justification for his actions. And once you get to know even the 'worst' people, they show themselves to be made up of so much that is deemed good.

"Or perhaps I have weak instincts" Mira added to herself.

It no longer mattered anyway. She was no longer alone in this process. She would receive guidance when faced with the inner turmoil of trying to decide which action was the right or best one. A being far wiser would help her make the difficult decisions, show her the right way, help her in times of distress. She realised that even with nothing more, just having Pixie by her side to guide and support her, her world would already be much better, her choices wiser and her life more worth living.

Mira, for all her strengths, was fractured inside by lack of confidence in her own judgement and wisdom. She was great at questioning her every move and thought, owning all the blame, looking for her part, her fault in every outcome. Most of her relief perhaps came from the possibility of laying part of the responsibility, the main part of it, on someone else's shoulders.

She showered, got dressed and had her coffee. She was too excited to settle down to anything and waited anxiously for Pixie to appear, feeling impatient, looking forward to her adventure and yet nervous of what might lie ahead at the same time.

Pixie did appear, to Mira's immense relief, as soon as she had finished her morning ritual. Her warm glow spread first, followed by the twinkle and shine she brought into the room with her. "I'm ready" Mira thought.

After her usual full smile Pixie dived in straight away "I know where to take you first. You said you wanted to be happy always, all the time. So that's where we're going to go. To a world where everyone is always happy"

"Sounds perfect" Mira said. And what if I don't want to leave it?"

"I suppose you could wish for that" Pixie said. "But let me warn you straight away, I doubt you will wish that. And even if you did, I would advise against. But let's cross that bridge when we get to it"

"If we do" she added after a moment's pause.

"Okay. I'm ready"

"Close your eyes"

Mira obeyed.

Within an instant and after a bright flash, she heard Pixie's voice: "Open them"

Mira did. She was in a room that looked disappointingly familiar. In fact, had she moved at all?

She looked up at Pixie with questioning eyes.

"Yes, you have moved", Pixie seemed to have read her very thoughts." You're in a different world. I thought I'd ease you in. Your room is the same, but everything outside is different. I'm going to leave you now to investigate, but don't fear, I'm always by you, just ask a question and you'll hear my answer. If you need me to appear, simply wish it". And with that she was gone.

Mira got up slowly, she walked around her flat. Everything was exactly the same. "No point staying here" she thought and went downstairs. She stepped out into the same grey, cloudy, dense gloom she had expected to leave behind. Again she wondered at this. Happiness meant clear, bright skies, didn't it? "Obviously not" she told herself sternly. She refused to allow even a crumble of doubt against her newfound guardian angel to breeze into her heart. Doubts crept in all too easily with her. And that was inevitably followed by disappointment. She could not allow that. Pixie was her only hope.

But nature is habit and habit is stronger than will. Already the slight shadow of dark was sprinkling its heavy grey. As yet mild and too small, too inconsequential to have a real effect on Mira's attitude, and yet, there were the first glimmers of distress.

"For some reason I had pictured the 'happy' world to be bright with sunshine, sparkling, warm serene". And then a thought occurred to her that let Pixie off the hook and brought hope back in. "But maybe this is the point. The weather can't make us happy can it? Happiness comes from within. That's where I fail. It's me, not the weather that can make me happy or unhappy."

The thought satisfied her. It was all her fault after all. Her automatic go-to explanation for anything and everything that went wrong in life. Pixie would teach her how to become a better person.

And then a retort: "But sometimes the weather does lift or lower a mood", she thought. "At the very least, it has an effect on our moods".

"Stop fretting Mira" she told herself. "You haven't seen or experienced anything yet and already your mind has gone and written an entire essay. Be open to new experiences without dragging your usual analysing, judging brain into it."

As she started to look around her, her surprise grew. The street was dirty, far dirtier than the one she had left behind. There were piles of rubbish everywhere. It looked like it had not been cleaned for a very long time. She could see no one around. She started walking towards a cafe she often went to in her 'normal' world. And sure enough it was open. But there was no one inside, not even any employees. She walked back out, increasingly confused. None of this made any sense.

"Pixie, where is everybody?"

"They're happy" was the answer.

"You know what I mean. Where are they physically?"

"You'll see them soon"

Mira left it at that. She continued walking down the street until she heard music and laughter coming from somewhere. She followed the sounds and reached a tall building. The music was coming from one of the rooms on the first floor. She walked up and found the door wide open, so she entered.

It took her eyes a few moments to adjust to the bright light inside. It looked like the whole town was in that one, not very big, space. It was way too crowded, way too bright and way, way too loud. She stood by the door, tempted to make a fast exit. But her curiosity won over and she slowly started to make her way through the throng of people. Everyone seemed happy, that was obvious, at least on the surface. They were laughing, dancing, talking, shouting. Their faces shone brightly, all mouths curved up, eyes shining.

Mira felt overwhelmed by the sheer noise and airless density of people in the room. Nonetheless, she was drawn further in, her fists clenched slightly with determination. She would find out what she had been brought here to learn. She made her way over to the bar and stood there. No one was serving, not that she wanted a drink anyway. And in fact, she hadn't brought any money with her. Did they even use the same kind of money here? She had no idea.

She started watching the crowd. Again the thought struck her how happy everyone looked. A woman, laughing out loud as she approached, leaned against the bar next to her. "What's your name?" she shouted over the noise.

"Mira" Mira shouted back.

And that was it. No further questions followed, no introduction, not even an acknowledgement. The woman moved on.

"I don't understand", Mira thought. And she heard Pixie's reply "Join them"

Mira tried to obey. She moved away from the bar and joined a group that was dancing. But it was hard. She didn't feel happy herself and she hated crowds and noise. She tried to move to the music, but the music was not to her liking and even the loud music was being drowned out by the sounds of laughter and talk.

"I need some air", she thought and pushed her way back through the crowds to the door. It seemed to take her more time and effort to get out, than it had on her way in and she could feel herself start to panic. But before leaving, she took one last look around the room anyway and then practically ran out and back down the stairs. As soon as she was in fresh air once more she felt better.

"Pixie, I don't understand this at all. Can you explain?"

"Not really. It's better if you experience it. Just carry on Mira. Have some faith, and do please keep an open mind"

Perplexed, Mira decided to at least try to fully embrace her part.

The weather was not welcoming, but she neither wanted to go back to her flat, where there was nothing different, nor did she want to go back into the crowded party.

She trudged along down filthy streets, looking around her at times, but mostly looking down at the dirty pavement, lost in her own thoughts. It started to rain. She saw some seats that had been left outside in front of a cafe. There was enough shelter there for her to keep dry, so she took a seat. Someone else had obviously spotted the same temporary haven and was comfortably seated. Mira took refuge next to her. She felt irritated to see that she was seated next to another laughing, merry woman. Mira wondered what she was laughing at. She returned the woman's happy gaze with a smile, one that she didn't really feel inside. It felt fake and Mira was sure that was how it looked to the woman. Everything was so odd in this place.

"Hi" the woman said.

"Hi" Not knowing what else to say, "I'm Mira"

"I'm Regie. What a beautiful day", Regie turned her face back out to the rain. The conversation seemed to have come to an end with this person as soon as it had started. Mira was lost for words and her neighbour seemed to be lost in her own happy state of mind.

"Oh hell, what do I have to lose", she thought suddenly and turned back to Regie. "What do you do?"

"Oh, this and that. I sometimes work in the cafe, when I feel like it. I laugh and dance. There are so many parties and social gatherings, it's hard to find time to do anything else." She laughed again.

"Why is there so much rubbish around?"

Regie shrugged. "We had this idea a while back to give a party and invite everyone in town, so we could all have fun together. It's been so much fun though, no one has left it yet except to snatch some food or sleep, only to return again. It'll get cleaned." And with that she was off in her own world again.

"But, by who?"

Regie shrugged again. It was obviously a question that had not occurred to her and now that it was out there, not knowing the answer did not seem to bother her in the least. Mira was starting to feel exasperated. She still did not understand. "Is this what happiness is?" she asked out loud. The woman paid no attention. She did not even seem to notice, a happy smile was fixed onto her face, which was gazing out at the pouring rain.

But dear Pixie did notice. "Happiness is a state of mind Mira. It doesn't matter what the weather's like, how much rubbish piles on the streets, how crowded or noisy a place the person is in, people here will always feel happy. I could have created this world in what you would think of as a paradise, but what would be the point in that? The beauty of the place would blind you to the true nature of happiness. If you were in your perfect paradise Mira, soon enough you'd get bored, you'd find tiny faults at first, then major ones, and then eventually nothing worth striving for. One of the greatest strengths of humankind is its ability to adapt. In times of pain this is a lifesaver. You get used to the pain, the new way of life and still discover things worth living for, things that are beautiful, that bring you joy. The same is true for paradise. You'll adapt and find things you are not satisfied with, things you want to change, so you'll become dissatisfied and hence eventually unhappy again. Your nature, the law of the universe is impermanence, so if you're looking for 'happily ever after', well it doesn't exist, cause even paradise changes, in your mind if nowhere else, and it quickly becomes a place that is no longer paradise. But don't worry, you've yet to see a lot more and all the different pieces will eventually fit into place. Be patient"

What Pixie said made sense, but Mira was still stuck in the weirdness of what she had been experiencing. Stuck there, her questions continued: "But if they're happy, won't they want a beautiful place? Won't they live in harmony with nature? Wouldn't they all be running outdoors?"

"Honey, why would they? They're already happy wherever they are, whatever their surroundings. They have no need to make things better, or other than they already are. For them, this is paradise. And so is a lush forest, or war torn country for that matter. It's all the same to them. They're happy all the time, remember? That's what you wanted, wasn't it? Well, this is one way a world in which everyone is happy might look. They don't need to make things different. They don't care whether they work or not, or whether someone else works or not. It doesn't matter to them"

Mira felt more than a little bit cheated. Pixie had made them happy in circumstances where they could not have been. Or could they? She had magical powers after all. But she didn't want to argue back too strongly. She wasn't quite sure what she was thinking anyway. So she simply added: "I couldn't be happy here". It was a loaded question, in spite of the gentle way it had been offered.

"You're missing the point. It's not about being happy here, or somewhere else. They're not happy because they're here. They simply are happy"

"So if I asked to stay here, I would be happy and not wish for anything else?"

"Yes"

"Take me back Pixie. I'm not sure I want this. Then again, if I feel happy and nothing matters, maybe that's exactly what I want"

"I'm going to take you back Mira. You don't need to make that decision right now. Remember, you can always come back. Or in fact you could create your own perfect world and go there instead. But for now we need to go back. We haven't finished with your lessons yet. Be patient. Let me take you through a few more worlds. You might find your opinion changes. Things will become clearer with experience, don't you worry"

With a flash they were back in her flat.

"Is this the 'real' one?" asked Mira.

"In truth, it is as real as any other. But, yes, what you mean is, is this the world you've lived in for many years, so the answer is yes"

Mira pondered for a moment, then asked: "Ok so they have nothing to strive for, nothing seems to matter. But they're happy. Isn't that what we all want? Isn't that far better than this world in that sense? Maybe that's where I should be"

"You say that, because you don't yet understand why human beings suffer, what the whole point is. And in fact you don't understand what suffering is, or pain, or even unhappiness for that matter. Just be open. You will understand eventually, don't worry. See a few more things and stop analysing the experience you've just had with your mind. Just accept it and move on. You're doing your usual thing of thinking too hard, analysing too much. Do you realise that is just a tactic to distract you from what's really important, from where we really understand and know and gain wisdom? It's your heart I'm talking about Mira. You're focusing so hard on your mind that you escape from what your heart is really feeling. The heart doesn't create wrong tracks. It simply knows and what it knows is the truth. You're avoiding noticing what it already is feeling and could tell you if you remembered how to listen. Intuition is wiser than thinking. Intuition, as long as you know how to listen to it and hear it, will always guide you well. And true wisdom is born in the heart, which is wiser than both those. Stop over-thinking. Stop feeling that you need to understand clearly every single little detail of everything. True knowledge is like a spark, not the result of thinking over and over a complex equation. Thinking is only a small part of what leads to true wisdom. Let your body and soul feel the experience and then let it go. Let it settle without all the flags and bandages of labels, judgements and analysis. Those things tie the truth down, bind it, smother it. Let it breathe Mira. The experience is already a part of you. You don't need to cling to it, claw at it, pull it apart,... Just let it be"

Mira sighed. She felt tired and confused, but willing to obey.

"Now sleep" Pixie said. Mira looked up and thanked her. With that Pixie was gone. And sure enough, Mira went straight to bed and fell asleep within minutes, her brain exhausted from overworking, had instantly become a blank. She had a dreamless and thoroughly restful night.

It is not possible to numb ourselves towards only unpleasant feelings. We either become numb to the entire rainbow of human emotional possibility, or we experience both the joy and the sorrow, ideally both with grace.

"To be sensitive is to be alive" Vanda Scaravelli

The next morning Mira was waiting for Pixie when she appeared and she didn't pause for any pleasantries. Her question had been ready for a while and rushed out through her lips straight away. "So are you telling me that the point of all our suffering is so that we keep trying to improve ourselves and the world? To make things better, nicer, to progress?"

"No, not quite. In fact, no, that is not the point. However, without wisdom, what you think will bring you happiness only ends up bringing stagnation, which turns into dissatisfaction. It does not go deep and it cannot last. It cannot fulfil a searching soul. There would be nothing to wish for, or so you imagine. There is a point to it all dear Mira, but it's not something that can be explained. It needs to be experienced to be understood." She placed her hand on her heart, indicating where Mira needed to look. But Mira did not notice. As always, she was lost in her own thoughts.

"Here" Pixie added, touching Mira's heart gently, driving the point she was making through.

"There is a point to life and death. There's a point to joy and sorrow. And you will find out, there is beauty in sadness too. There is satisfaction in striving for better. What makes your world beautiful is precisely the mosaic of emotions all of you, every single one of you, experience. And yes, there is something beyond what you call happiness and unhappiness, something far more wonderful. And that *is* the point. To go beyond all of this, and to want to. But you need to realise all this for yourself and we have a lot more to experience together. Things will become clearer. Don't try to rush to conclusions. Just stay open"

Mira gazed at Pixie, taking in her words, trying to feel them, rather than think them.

"Okay, I'm ready for what's next" she said. And she was, with less doubt and less anxiety this time…

When Mira opened her eyes the first thing she became aware of was the air. It felt stifled and stagnant. She felt and knew, but as soon as her usual self doubt crept in, decided that she thought, she had landed in the middle of a city of sorts. All around her were tall buildings. She could see wide, smoothly asphalted roads and pavements, tall signs and lights everywhere. Then it struck her how clean everything was. There was not a single bit of litter in sight. But then, neither was there a single tree or plant within sight either.

A plane rushed by above her, its loud engine sending rumbling vibrations all around.

This was certainly different. Very different from where she came from and the first truly 'other' world she had experienced.

She started to wander down the street. Every window was a shop, cafe, bar or restaurant. "I must be on the main street", she thought to herself. She turned off onto the next street she came across. She had chosen not to enter any of the cafes or bars, because she didn't feel ready to speak to anyone just yet. She wanted to see a little more of the city she had landed in first. The street she ended up walking down was very similar to the one she had just left. Wide street with high rises either side and broad pavements without a glimpse of anything green anywhere, and every ground floor window a shop, cafe or restaurant.

Walking down it, gazing about, she saw a shop sign advertising legal services. It struck her, because it stood out from the rest. "Or a service business", she thought, "I'll add it to my list". She was trying to be sarcastic. Something about the place just did not feel right. There was so much public business going on and yet no public in sight... She had not come across a single pedestrian during her wandering yet.

She kept turning in and out of different streets. And to her befuddlement, each one looked exactly the same as the other.

Eventually she stopped in front of a cafe. She gazed through the window. It seemed quite enough. She walked in. There was a couple sitting at one table and a few others dotted around the place sitting alone. She found a table not too far from the couple, so that she could maybe overhear them speak and find out a little more about where she was. But then again, she did not want to be too close either. She did not want to impose her presence on them, and neither did she feel confident enough to take the risk of being imposed upon herself.

The couple were talking about someone they obviously both knew well. It was the usual kind of gossip and held absolutely no interest for Mira. She looked around for a menu, but suddenly remembered she did not have any money on her. "Great oversight, Mira" she mumbled to herself. She decided she would need to leave before anyone came up to her to take her order. She was feeling embarrassed already. She wished she had thought of details like that before she came here. As she started to stand up, she noticed her bag sitting on the seat next to hers. Her first thought was, "I didn't bring this with me". Then, straight away "I don't even know if they use the same currency here anyway, or even if they do, whether I have enough". It had occurred to her that she might be in the future. Even though she had not yet spoken to anyone or even really seen anything, she was convinced she had set herself up to fail and was feeling thoroughly disheartened. A city more developed than any she had ever seen, maybe more advanced, maybe better, maybe not...

She decided to take a look in 'her' bag. It wasn't as if anything that had been happening to her was normal anyway. Simply appearing here in a flash was anything but normal. Perhaps

Pixie had arranged her bag to appear. Hadn't she wished it after all? Only a passing thought, but still, it was a wish to not embarrass herself and to be able to pay, and experiencing all aspects of life here was in line with her purpose.

So she sat back down and started looking through her bag. There were the usual odds and ends she kept with her: lip salve, hand cream, purse, phone, notebook and pen. "What use is my phone to me here" she thought with sarcasm. She opened her purse and sure enough, it was full of money, and, to her joy, not any currency she recognised. Well, it had appeared out of nowhere, so the currency must be right. She was sure she had whatever she needed for any situation. If not, she could simply wish for it. Those details were obviously not meant to concern her. Everything necessary would fall into place. She could relax and focus on finding out more about this place and its people.

"And don't worry about getting into trouble or making a fool of yourself" she thought , "you can always wish yourself back to safety". So she relaxed and looked around for a menu, but still could not see anything resembling one.

Her attention drifted back to the couple nearby. Their conversation had moved on to their respective jobs. They were becoming increasingly animated. Mira got the sense that neither particularly enjoyed what they were doing. They were both complaining about how hard they needed to work and they could not agree on a time and day that was mutually convenient. So they were arguing. They were both too busy and they simply could not agree on a time that suited them both without any inconvenience, so a compromise was necessary, at least by one of them, and neither was giving an inch. Mira thought they were going to break into argument any moment, but they didn't. Instead they said they'd call and left any next meeting and its details to some possible vague future.

She didn't see either pay and no one came to clear their table.

She cast her mind back over their conversation. The snippets she had heard weren't enough for her to piece together what either did, but she guessed they worked in offices. "Not enough, I still have no idea" she thought, but with little else to go on, she gave up.

She also gave up on being served and decided to leave. She couldn't see any point staying there any longer. There was no one to listen to or talk with, she wasn't hungry, she might as well leave. She took one last look around, picked up her bag and walked out.

She continued to wander aimlessly around the streets for a while, but she was beginning to feel tired. All this wandering around felt pointless and sapped her energy. She had to discover a way of finding out what she'd come here to learn. She felt a pressing need to keep moving, anything would do, it didn't really matter what. She felt timid and unsure, but she reminded herself that she could wish herself back at any time. She took a deep breath in and entered another cafe that was busy, bracing herself against the noise and clamour as she walked through its automatic glass doors. She found a table and sat down. It was louder in here. Groups, couples and people sitting alone spread out around tables. She watched them as they talked, ate and drank. Once more she saw no one serving.

A couple walked through the door and Mira watched them make their way over to a cluster of terminals to the left of the entrance. She focused her attention on them, watching with curiosity. They spent some time at one of these terminals and used the screen. It was a touch screen, like some kind of advanced game console. The young man took a card out of his pocket. They then moved further along to their left, chatting away happily between themselves. A machine opened up and two cups of coffee and something like a pastry appeared on a tray. The male picked the tray up and the female led them over to an empty table. "So that's how it's done", thought Mira, "no wonder I've seen no one serve. There's no need for people here".

She didn't feel much like eating or drinking anything yet and it didn't seem to matter whether she did or not, so she remained seated, looking around her, searching for something interesting to watch or listen to. She started to listen in on the conversation the group nearest her were having. They were discussing some event. There were four of them, three men and a woman. They all looked like they were in their early thirties, although it was hard to be sure. The woman wore so much make up, her face was a mask and the mask could have been hiding deep grooves in her face or a healthy young complexion. Her eyes looked tired though. Even the men had make up on, although their faces were not covered quite so thickly with it. They could have been fifty or even twenty for that matter.

One of the men was disagreeing with what another one had just said: "That is utter nonsense. How could she? She'll never get away with it"

The woman piped in "but she has so far, and she will, mark my words. I bet any one of you that she will still be there in a year's time"

"Well" the first one replied, "a year is not too bad. As long as it stays at that. Chances are she'll go on and on though. Isn't that what usually ends up happening?"

They were all quiet for a moment.

Then another guy looked up "Hey Joe, what happened with that arsehole boss of yours? Is he still fighting that lawsuit?"

"With everything's he's got" replied Joe, the last one of the four. "And he will continue to. The man's made of brass. No sense of shame. But then again, you can't help but admire him. He's had every law book thrown at him. They've been at it for years, tried everything possible, and yet he's still there, working away, making shed loads of money, brazenly advertising the fact he's rich through dubious means, but somehow his lawyers have him covered. I don't think they'll ever find something that will stick. Ever" He went back to his drink gloomily.

"Good on him" the first guy remarked. "Which one of you would not want to be in his place?"

The woman gazed up, a spark of disagreement rising to her lips, but only for a moment. The lips twitched, wouldn't she really? Her lips settled into a grimace of distaste. She looked down at the table, embarrassed. It was obvious to Mira that she had decided she would.

At a neighbouring table a man was complaining about some machine malfunctioning again. Mira guessed it to be a home device from the way he was speaking, but she could not figure out what it might be.

A couple a few tables down got up and carried their trays over to the right of the door, depositing the rubbish and tray before exiting.

"Well someone must collect the rubbish and prepare the food somewhere, surely" Mira thought, but she was not that certain. Perhaps in this futuristic place they had created machines did all that too.

Suddenly she was curious. What would the food taste like? Did it smell? She had seen films based on future life and the food in them was always processed, made not for taste but for the optimum mix of nutrients which were added chemically... She decided to try it. She got up and walked over to the machine the first couple had used. The screen was black. She looked for a switch but saw none. She touched the screen and sure enough it lit up. There were too many options for her to get her head around. She decided to make a random selection. After all, the point was to taste anything, whatever, she didn't have a clue and it didn't matter. She kept touching the screen until an option lit up, then she touched finish. An amount appeared on the screen with no indication of currency. She pressed pay. She could not see anywhere where she could deposit notes or coins. The couple had paid by card. I wish I had a card that works, she thought. She opened her purse and sure enough there was a card.

She could not see a slot for the card either. She touched the card to the screen itself. Nothing. She saw a red light in the right lower corner and touched her card there. It worked. She moved on to the next terminal and picked up the tray that appeared and then wandered over to a table in a different part of the room. What she had on her tray looked odd. She could not tell whether it was sweet or savoury. She took a bite. It was surprisingly tasty for such a bland looking thing. But she still couldn't tell what it was or what it was meant to taste like.

The two women at the adjacent table were speaking too quietly for her to pick out much of their conversation. There was a woman sitting along at the table opposite hers and a group of three men to her right. She started listening to the men.

"That's never going to work" one was saying.

Another replied "how else do you propose we make money?"

"Not that way. We'll never be rich that way. And anyway, it's not so…" his gaze trailed off, the sentence unfinished.

"So what if it's not so glamorous or flashy?" His friend seemed to find the right words for him. "That's what you were trying to say, isn't it? Does it matter? As long as we make more money I couldn't care less. We can tell people whatever we like. Make up a glamorous job for yourself if you like. We want to make money and this is the best plan we've come up with so far. I say we stick to it"

Mira started to feel bored. Her chest started to weigh in on itself, heavy and dense. "I think I've had enough. This place is depressing me" she thought. The conversations were bringing her down. The energy of the people around her was low and heavy. The air in the room was heavy. She needed some air. She got up abruptly and left in a hurry, completely forgetting about her tray and was stunned to hear an automated voice behind her say "Please remove your tray and dispose of the rubbish. Thank you" After a moments awkward hesitation she returned to her table and picked up her tray. A few people had turned around to watch her, with little interest. She deposited the tray and its contents as she had seen the couple do and walked out.

Had the table spoken? Were there CCTV cameras around? Obviously something had triggered an automatic message. Was it because she walked away from the table while sensors felt the presence of the tray on it? What on earth was this place?

She felt distraught and decided she needed to find a park, or at least a green square or garden. She needed to breathe.

She walked around the streets, much faster now. She realised suddenly that she couldn't see a single tree, or flower, or anything green or natural anywhere in sight. In fact, now that she thought about it, she hadn't seen a single green thing since appearing in this world. She was starting to feel claustrophobic. She wondered if she should wish herself back, but that didn't seem right. She had understood practically nothing about this place and she felt she had seen too little.

She spent another hour, or maybe longer, all sense of time had left her, walking around, looking for space, greenery, anywhere she could breathe and gather her thoughts. Having still not found anything green and feeling utterly exasperated, tired, spent, frustrated and annoyed she cried "Pixie, I wish to be back. Is it time? Oh please help me." Her main frustration was with herself and her failure to understand or learn anything from where she had been placed. She was letting Pixie down by admitting defeat and running out, but she could not bear it any longer.

In a flash she was back in her room. She took a few deep breaths, ran over to her window and stuck her head out into the cold, fresh air. Only after she had had her fill did she turn around to see Pixie watching her.

"I'm sorry Pixie. I know I chickened out too soon. I couldn't understand. But I couldn't stand it any longer either. That place was suffocating. I had to leave" She shuddered as she remembered the grey, heavy world of cement.

"Oh you got the message alright" Pixie replied. "You're trying to understand too much with your head as usual. Trying to analyse and make sense of everything is fine at times, but this is not the time. All the detail you could have gathered in that world would not help you as much as your instincts and what you felt while there. Stop thinking and feel"

"It was horrible, unnatural. The people felt, I don't know, like they were, I don't know, unnatural I suppose"

"No heart?"

Pixie had struck a chord, Mira looked up, her face lightening a little, but then "No, that doesn't make sense. How could I know? I never spoke to any one of them"

"But you felt their energy. Just as you would get a sense of a person in this world, watching, sensing, feeling. You need to trust your instincts more"

"I suppose. I don't know. They had a cold energy. Repressed. Forced down. Everything was so heavy. The energy felt caved in and dark. And all those masks. And no green, oh God, no green at all. They were driven maybe. That word comes to my mind, determined, but cold. Yes, I suppose that's lack of heart in a way. And there was nothing green, Pixie" The last sentence, a repetition, came out as a moan, Mira's distress of the past few hours were returning with force. She could feel anguish throughout her body. And again, she repeated "It was horrible"

But, in Pixie's presence, in the room with air blowing in through the open window, with the sense of security and time, her heart started to ease. And as the anguish retreated, increasingly, her brain took forestage. Questions started to appear in Mira's mind, they were flowing in faster and faster until there were so many of them…

"Pixie, what kind of a world was that? Is it the future? Is that what we create? And what do people do? It sounded like all they wanted in life was to get rich, no matter by what means. And is anyone poor? Have they at least figured out how to eradicate homelessness? And all the masks. Do they feel? Do they still cry? What's the food made of? Who makes it and clears it away? And…" she stopped, forcing herself to slow down.

"What do you think honey? Do you think they've eradicated poverty and homelessness?"

Mira only had to pause for a second. "No. The group was talking about getting rich. They wouldn't care if no one was poor and everyone was content. Besides, someone can only be rich in comparison…. But perhaps the poor are not homeless or hungry?"

"Honey, you said yourself, lack of heart. Don't you think there will be some people out there who don't make it?"

"I didn't see any"

"Remember how spotlessly clean all the streets were. Can you not guess?"

"They get cleaned away as well as all the rubbish?" Mira asked. She was making an attempt at humour. But Pixie's expression halted her forced chuckle mid throat. "Oh God, that's exactly what happens isn't it? They value appearance, wealth, but not humans, or nature, or animals I expect. So just like the contents of a dirty tray the poor and the homeless get cleaned away. But what happens to them?"

"They're disposed of. Literally. Think about it Mira. No value for human life. Why would they even lock them up? It would require money; to feed them, to keep them warm and locked up and clean, to monitor them, and all else that comes with that. There are no jails or shelters in that world. Once a person is convicted of a crime, he or she also gets disposed of. But those with money fight to the end. Money is everything in that world. It doesn't matter whether someone's guilty or innocent, if they have enough money, they can survive, if not, well, disposal eventually. Remember the talk about that rich guy fighting the lawsuits? They were sure he'd win. His morality didn't come into it. They weren't discussing what he'd done and whether he was guilty. In fact they all know he is guilty. It's not about doing right or wrong or abiding by the law, it's about making enough money so that you can be above the law. You called it the world of cement. You could call it the world of money. All of the worst of capitalism taken to an extreme."

"What about enjoyment? Love, happiness, fun?"

"They're too busy making money. They pay others to relax them, keep them healthy, whatever they want, as quickly as possible. You can't waste any time on such pursuits if every moment you spend on pleasure is a moment less spent on making money."

"World and hearts of money and cement. That sums it up then. You're right. I didn't need to stay there any longer"

And as with the day before, Pixie left Mira to rest and let her experience settle. Mira fell into a deep, dreamless sleep.

Everything has consequences, both the actions we choose to perform and the choice we make not to act. An environment that is unhappy harms everyone in it. None of us live in isolation and separate from our surroundings.

"Fulfil all your duties; action is better than inaction. Even to maintain your body, Arjuna, you are obliged to act. Selfish action imprisons the world. Act selflessly, without any thought of personal profit." Krishna to Arjuna in the Bhagavad Gita, III: 8-9, translation by Eknath Easwaran

She woke up feeling refreshed and happy in spite of the heaviness she had carried with her into her sleep. What a wonderful feeling this was, waking up in anticipation of what the new day might bring… Pixie had brought back the sense of anticipation and joy for life she had felt upon awakening every morning as a child. Gradually her mornings had become duller, but now once again, every day brought with it a new adventure and was full of potential. Every day came with excitement, learning and the experience of another unknown world. And plus Pixie was always there, supporting Mira each step of the way. Mira was excited about what this new day and yet another new world might bring. But before she could embark on a new adventure, she still had questions she needed answered from her previous experience. She got herself ready and settled to wait for Pixie, who appeared soon after Mira started to get fidgety and impatient.

"Pixie, did that world have governments? Had they at least found a way to live without war?

"They have governments of sorts, more like chief executives if you like. Businessmen, running their allotted areas like they would a company, with efficiency and profit in mind. Or they supposedly are, as efficiently as they can.

But corruption seeps into any organisation that holds power. In a society where money is power and power is money and in the culture the only aim is to get rich, earn more, amass more by whatever means necessary, it is inevitable I suppose. The stated aim of these chief executives is to help people make money and protect those that do. Their aims do not include taking care of the needy or finding ways to improve their situation and make them less needy. It's cheaper to get rid of them you see, and that way there are more jobs and resources left for those who already have wealth. They are in the eyes of the people the more deserving ones. As for wars, the people in that world realised at some point that war was a waste of their resources and time, so wars were kind of phased out"

"But that's wonderful Pixie!" Mira exclaimed. "At least there's something positive about the place. But what about people feeling aggression, anger, hatred? What about the greedy wanting to take over resources from other areas to become richer and more powerful? What about those who don't get rich, do they not revolt? Do they not get together and fight back?"

"Any that fall through the cracks are dealt with too quickly to be able to get together. Those who haven't fallen through yet spend their entire time, energy and mental power on working on how to get rich, rather than how to make the lives of those like themselves better or how to resolve inequality. As for aggression, hatred and anger, they are feelings and people in that world are numb to feelings. Feelings, they decided long ago, slow progress, compassion creates disquiet, depression decreases efficiency. So they found ways of numbing feelings, squashing them down, getting rid of them. So no, there's not much of anger, but again, if any surfaces, it is dealt with swiftly and efficiently. Feelings are not tolerated and there are not many who would be willing to face death in an attempt to voice their feelings publicly. There are plenty of narcotics around to deal with any emotions that might surface. No risks are taken. It's not about 'living' with feelings, excitement, joy, it's all about money and living with whatever money provides"

"It's a bit extreme. I can't imagine anyone deadening to their feelings so much that they never search for laughter, contentment or happiness. I suppose I still don't really understand"

"That's because you're trying to understand in your body, with your feelings and your current mindset. It's a completely different world after all. You just need to accept that that's the way they have chosen to be"

"But isn't that somehow dead?"

"Compared to your rich mosaic of emotions, yes. I never suggested it was better. It's just different."

"Do they not fall in love?"

"What do you think?"

"No, I suppose not, it's a deep emotion. You can't have depth of feeling in positive ways without also allowing in the difficult and dark and you can't numb some emotions without numbing them all. But then how do couples get together? They obviously do"

"Just like partners get together when creating a new business venture. They find someone they are compatible with, in terms of work, wealth, mindset, and they form a partnership. They procreate and build their own family, as if building their business. It all fits in and is pretty simple really"

"Well, it's certainly not a world that attracts me in any way" Mira concluded.

"You have more to see and gradually your experiences will build into something more tangible. Now, are you ready for the next one?"

Mira sighed, took a deep breath and replied "Yes, I'm ready"

When she opened her eyes, the first thing she noticed was the warm sun on her skin, followed swiftly by a sharp unpleasant smell. She wrinkled up her nose and covered it with her hand, which made hardly any difference at all.

She had landed in an impoverished street, or world maybe. The buildings looked old and in desperate need of cleaning up. They were dirty and cracked with whole corners or areas of them fallen off. The windows were gaping holes, any glass that they used to hold long gone. There was rubbish lying around everywhere, not even gathered in piles or even in bags, just dumped haphazard all over the place. As her eyes got increasingly used to the bright light and she was able to see more, a sense of horror spread through her. The dilapidated pavements were crawling with people. Everywhere around her there were filthy, smelly people in dirty, old, torn clothes. The people reeked. The clothes reeked. The rubbish reeked. Everything smelt bad and rotten.

No one stood straight or walked tall. People were bent over double, most of them looking through trash, presumably to find something to eat. Some were lying around on the sides of pavements. Some had managed to find some shelter in door entrances. They looked like they were too weak or ill to move at all. They all looked listless, not a smile on a face, and from what Mira could see, they had no visible reason to smile anyway.

She started slowly and carefully walking down the street. The pavement was so broken up, full of cracks and potholes, in parts it had been worn down to no more than dirty gravel. The sun seemed out of place in the sky that looked over this world. She had a desire to get away, a very strong one, and yet she persevered. She had been brought here to learn something and she was determined to learn as much as she could about this world. She wanted to know why it had fallen on such hard times and how the people lived. She wondered if there were rich and clean streets in this city or whether it was all in a state of decay. The rubbish came from somewhere, so there must be people somewhere who could afford to buy and eat food before disposing of their rubbish in the streets.

She couldn't muster up the courage to speak to anyone, not just yet. The people around her were lost in their own world, weighed down by their poverty and troubles, pains and fears.

She felt concern for them and sadness. What an unhappy place, she thought. Her limbs felt tired walking on these streets. She had grown accustomed to the smell already though and barely noticed it. She felt too tired to walk on, but did not want to stop or sit, feeling out of place and uncomfortable. She looked down at her own clothes and to her surprise, she was dressed in a similar way, dirty, torn, faded clothes hanging off her limbs. No wonder no one paid her any attention. "Well done", she thought to herself, "thanks Pixie". Then it occurred to her that she could always ask for guidance.

"Pixie", she thought, "guide me to where I can learn more. I think I've experienced enough of this street". She noticed she was nearing the end of the street, and she abruptly came to a halt in front of a barbed wire fence.

Beyond the fence were tall trees, blocking any further views from her sight. She walked up to them and tried to get a glimpse of what lay behind them. She saw parts of a well-kept garden and through a gap between the trees she caught a glimpse of a grand building with white washed, brightly coloured window frames and intricate awnings. In spite of the bright colours and picture of warmth, it looked foreboding.

"Don't waste your energy", the voice came from right behind her. She turned round to see an old man looking up at her from his half-bent position. Or was he even old? He was covered in dirt and mud, his clothes were nearing full disintegration, it was hard to tell what age he was. He could have been far younger in years than his looks suggested. His mouth was a gaping hole, most of his teeth had fallen out, and what still remained was rotting in his mouth.

"They beat beggars away. You'd think they could throw some crumbs at you, but even their garbage is too good for us"

"Who lives there?"

At this the man looked puzzled. "Where have you come from?" He didn't care for an answer though. "The mayor, his holiness, the saviour of our city, our shining beacon" he added with a smirk, disgust and anger showing on his face.

"Is there no help for us?" Mira asked, searching in her mind for the right questions.

"Things get worse, and worse, and just as you think they can't get any worse, they get worse still" he replied.

He was becoming interested in this stranger. Who could possibly not know the mayor and not know how hopeless their situation was.

"Tell me about him" Mira said

"What's there to tell", boredom replaced what little animation the man's face had shown. "Same old"

When he saw that Mira was still waiting, a thought occurred to him, "Do you have anything to eat?"

Mira looked down at her clothes and spread her hands. So far whenever she had needed anything in these worlds, it had appeared in her bag, but this time she had no bag. Then she noticed pockets in her rags and dipped her hands into them, hoping in her heart that what she needed would appear. She could not face the idea of disappointing this poor man. Sure enough, she pulled out a large piece of bread. She handed it over to him without thinking.

"Wow, where did you get that?" He was excited. He grabbed the bread quick as lightning and pulled it to his chest as if it was the greatest treasure in the world, one which he was terrified of losing. He looked around them speedily, afraid someone else might have seen the handover. "Fights over food must be common", Mira thought. "And no wonder. These people are starving."

"Come" the man said and practically pushed her into a street opposite. It also turned out to be a dead end. He crouched by a broken down doorway and started to eat the piece of bread with gusto. Mira watched and waited until he was finished. He was too consumed with feeding himself, trying to satisfy one of his most basic needs, to have any interest in holding a conversation.

When he finished he looked up. The bread could not have satisfied him, it wasn't big enough, and yet he looked like it had. He was more relaxed and a vague smile was animating his lips.

"You don't know anything and you turn up with food. And you give it to me" he remarked, obviously most surprised by his last observation. Mira wondered whether she should have shared it with him, rather than handing the whole piece over. She had aroused his suspicion. But then, she did not need it and he so very much did. She let the thought pass.

"Are there a lot of rich people?" she asked. "Is everyone poor and hungry? What's happened to the streets and buildings? What do you do?"

"Hah. What do we do… We die!" he stated, as if it was the most obvious thing in the world. And perhaps it was, Mira realised.

"Yes, there are those who are rich, but not many. Thousands, millions, of us against a handful of them. They protect themselves with walls and wires and guns. And we're too destitute and weak to do anything about it, which is probably why they keep us this way. A starving man has no strength to fight.

It used to be different you know. We tried to rise up in the early days. To take back what was ours. To defend our rights. But they were smart. They worked subtly for a long time and no one noticed what was happening until it was too late. Very quickly we were dying of disease, hunger, crime. The population fighting within itself, everyone at each others' throats. Too busy to notice the world disintegrate around us, while they" he pointed towards the fenced building, spitting at the word 'they', "did their worst. By the time we realised what was happening, it was too late. They were protected, comfortable and fed, holding utmost power throughout the world and we had nothing. Nothing at all. Not even a piece of bread"

He was speaking more freely now, so Mira did not interrupt with questions and listened to him intently. She noticed how well spoken he was and it occurred to her that he must have had a good education earlier on in his life.

"It's too late now", listlessness returned to his face and body. He had run out of steam. "Too late. We watched it happen, too lazy to do anything about it, too stupid to notice and now we're paying the price"

Mira could think of nothing to say, so she watched his face and waited, but he had lost interest.

After a long silence, she asked "but there are so many of you" and realising her mistake she quickly corrected herself before she continued "us, and so few of them, surely it's possible to do something"

"We tried when we were stronger and still had hope and ideas, and even then we failed. Now we're nothing but dissipate stray cats, ravaging for food, too hungry, tired and weak to get together. Who cares? No one does anymore. There's no future for us."

"But even the rich need food, for that they need farms, factories. They need guards. What about the people who work for them?"

"Slaves. Those lucky enough to get work toil the soil or work the machines sixteen, eighteen hours a day. All they get is some measly food, enough so that they are able to continue with their work, not enough to gather strength and courage. They're never given free time anyway. They work or sleep. They have nowhere to talk. Any talk of unfairness, or change and they're done for. They're glad to be fed and clothed, beyond that, they don't care. Hell, I don't care and there was a time when I was one of those who led the movements. I led the uprising against these murderers. But those times have past. Now all I want is to die in peace with the least amount of pain. A person has nothing when he has lost all hope. Without hope, there is nothing."

"You said they did it subtly over many years. What did they do?"

"Where are you from?" his suspicion was increasing. Maybe he was wondering if she was a spy. Or maybe an alien, she realised looking at the incredulous expression on his face.

"Far away" she replied and glanced away, up the street at the dirt and poverty. Her soul ached.

"Why not" he seemed to resign himself to the idea that she was ignorant, or even if not, he was beyond caring.

He slumped down against the wall and she did the same.

"We elected those bastards. Hah. Most of us did. Not me. No. I knew they were crooks. But even I didn't see this coming, none of us did" He looked around, anger rising in his voice. "We did this to ourselves. Who would vote for their own destruction? We did. We threw away our lives, our rights. We said, here, take it all, you have it, we're too stupid to have these rights. Look we'll prove it to you by electing you and handing everything over, even our freedom, with our own hands.

They persuaded the people to turn against each other. They said they would beat crime and poverty" at this he laughed, a bitter, angry laugh.

"They said give us more power and we'll sort everything out. You unhappy? You discontented? Vote for us. We'll bring change. And that they did. Wars increased, unnecessary, stupid wars, wasted lives. Taxes went up. Benefits, work, support dwindled. They broke down the education system and made the hospitals too poor to function. They cut out the support system and the poor got furious. Crime increased. People got angry. They got heavy handed, using people's discontentment as an excuse to squash them with force. And those with work, those slightly better off wanted a better world, but instead of putting things right, instead of repairing a broken system, they swallowed the words of ego driven, selfish, short sighted, uncaring politicians whole. The politicians said, the government has no money for social care, for schools and hospitals. But then they waged wars. The prisons got fuller. They said, why feed criminals and brought back the death sentence to create space. They said these countries threaten our way of life and went to war. They said now we need full power, things aren't going well and declared a state of emergency. And each step we watched and cheered them on. We got poorer, they got richer, but we didn't notice. Those of us who noticed could do nothing. If we got caught, we vanished in the justice system, killed, never heard of again. If we didn't get caught, not many listened to us anyway.

When we started to ask questions and rise up, they brought the armies back from their pointless wars and unleashed them on us. For decades we continued to struggle and fight. But more of us died, were taken away, lost jobs, went hungry, became ill. Each year there were less of us fighting, with diminishing strength and hope, and more of us destitute and dying. Year by year it got worse. Until there was nothing left"

He looked up at her and then around. "Welcome to our world" he added. He was obviously done with his speech and his expression made it clear to Mira that further questions were not welcome. Yet Mira had so much to ask. She hesitated, but he had turned away, tired, hopeless, defeated, his anger without an outlet bubbling inside of him, demanding to be let out, but without any will left to boil or rise, there only to drain his energy.

She leaned against the wall, lost in her own thoughts. She noticed him leave and looked up, but his back was already turned to her and she let him go.

Could this really happen? Could a world destroy itself to such an extent? How many times she had felt that people in her own world seemed so excited to rush towards self destruction. But she had never taken that thought too seriously. And yet looking around her now, she wondered. She could see it was possible.

She wondered if she needed to stay on. She felt like a weakling, wanting so much to escape. But she could always come back if she wanted to. "I'd like to see this world from the other point of view" she thought, looking in the direction of the one decent house she had seen there. "How can they be surrounded with so much suffering and yet continue to live and act the way they do? How did they get to where they are now? What kind of people are these?"

For a moment she knew her heart was not in it. She felt disgusted by them already and she hadn't even caught a single glimpse of any one of them. On the other hand, she wanted to learn. She wanted to experience what made a person act the way they did. How could anyone shut down their conscience, their soul, their eyes to such an extent. "But first I need to rest", she thought.

She opened her eyes in her own room, Pixie was smiling down on her as she lay in bed. She sat up with a start.

"I need to go back there Pixie. Can I return, but this time to that house?"

"Yes darling. But don't you think you should rest first?"

"No. I need to go now. I need to understand. I could not rest with all that's on my mind."

"So be it" Pixie said with a smile. A bright flash followed and Mira, with her eyes firmly shut, was transported back.

She found herself in a richly decorated large room. Intricate carvings hung from the ceiling and the tops of the walls. Sunlight streamed through tall Victorian windows. A lace curtain danced in the breeze. She could hear birdsong coming from just outside the window. The room was decorated sumptuously; antiques, glittering silver, large, intricately framed mirrors and bright coloured cloths and hangings surrounded her.

A king size bed took up the centre of the wall across from her. The covers were piled up on one side and a young woman was mid conversation. Mira suddenly realised the conversation was directed at her. She looked down at herself and saw she was wearing a simple but clean maid's outfit. With a start she focused her attention on the woman, trying to figure out what she might have missed and what was being said.

"And don't overcook the coffee as you did yesterday. It was too bitter to drink. I had to get Maria to make a fresh batch."

Mira heard disdain and anger in the woman's voice. "And for God's sake hurry up with the bed. You know I hate an untidy room. Where is my brush?" Anger rising further, along with the pitch and volume of her voice.

"Sorry" Mira muttered, a little bewildered, looking around frantically for a brush, which turned out to be hiding in plain sight right beside the woman on a beautifully carved mango wood dresser. Perfumes and toiletries adorned the dresser, as well as a gold framed oval mirror. She took a few large steps to the dresser and leaned across the woman to reach for the brush. In her haste she nearly dropped it, but managed to grab it without a mishap in the end, although her movements felt ridiculous and quite clumsily.

"God you're slow. And useless" The last remark was uttered with emphasis. Mira got the clear impression it was meant to convey "and useless means out, and onto the streets"

"Sorry" she uttered again, not knowing how else to respond.

"Now get going, give me the brush, make the bed and get some coffee, and fast"

Mira obeyed, surprised at the audacity in the woman's treatment of her and increasingly annoyed. Once the bed was made and she had made a hasty escape, she pulled the door behind her and looked both ways along the corridor, not knowing which way to turn. She decided to follow her instincts, which duly led her to an extremely large kitchen. Cooks and maids were running around frantically. Someone pushed passed her, barely noticing her existence. She dared not ask where to make coffee, where to find it or what to do. The atmosphere was tense and heavy. The kitchen was airy enough, but somehow she couldn't breathe.

The chaos in the kitchen was overwhelming, yet she found everything she needed eventually, constantly feeling as if she was in everyone's way. No one paid her much attention. They were all consumed with their own work and they moved around tense and full of anxiety.

In spite of all the commotion and the high number of workers in the kitchen, they were still somehow managing to keep it spotless clean. Mira thought of the huge contrast this picture portrayed compared to the world inhabited by the people outside. It might as well have been on a different planet or in a completely different age.

Inviting smells were spreading from where pots and pans stood on a stove. But Mira knew she could not linger. She prepared the coffee as fast as she was able to and returned to her mistress' room. It seemed to take her ages to find her way. The building was massive, with corridors leading in all directions, people rushing around, doors opening and closing, giving her small glimpses into a life full of opulence and luxury. It occurred to her that if she was not able to find the right room, or if anyone asked her who she was or what she was doing, she would be lost. She had no idea what her mistress was called, or what her position in the house was. But, with Pixie's help, she reached the right door and entered.

While she'd been gone, her mistress had dressed herself beautifully. Her hair was tied back and she was sitting at her dresser applying make-up, gazing at herself intently in the mirror. Her expression suggested that she was well aware of her beauty.

It occurred to Mira that it must be very difficult for anyone from this house to step outside the boundaries marked by the wall and wired fence. They would be pounced on in an instant. Or would they? So much of this world was beyond her understanding. Maybe these people had convinced the population that any harm or even inconvenience caused to the powerful would result in so much pain, people stayed away without the need for any force or protection. But they had nothing to lose. Why would they not harass the people responsible for all their suffering? Even if it was only to snatch a piece of clothing and run.

Was each trip outside a huge military undertaking? What did this woman do with her time? In spite of all her wealth, was she not in a way, no more than a prisoner in her own home?

Her thoughts were scattered away by the orders that were being issued from the woman's direction and Mira did her best to listen and obey.

"And don't forget, Sir John is coming for lunch. I will look amazing for that" The message Mira received was "and you will make that happen", barely covering the hidden threat of you'll regret it if I find so much as the tiniest fault in your preparations. Her mistress seemed to talk only in a threatening and disdainful tone. Mira wondered whether this tone was used only on the servants, or if she always spoke this way. Perhaps her beauty, together with her wealth and position, gave her this bizarre sense of entitlement.

"Now leave me alone. And make sure you don't waste any more time". Mira moved towards the door, with no clue as to what she was to do next. Presumably she had a routine, chores to complete, something to do, but none of these were things she was familiar with and she wisely chose not to make any enquiries.

She left the room and as she had no idea where else to go she decided to return to the kitchen.

The kitchen was just as busy as when she had left it. She saw a maid eat a piece of stale bread in the corner. With all the appetising food all round the kitchen, Mira was surprised to see this. Surely at least these people were given proper food? But in this world any level of deprivation and immorality seemed possible. As before, everyone was too busy to pay attention to her and she had no idea how to talk to any of them. None seemed inviting. She felt utterly lost and useless.

Someone glanced at her at last, but with disdain and perhaps some pity. Not doing anything was criminal and the punishment was what? The streets? Death? Mira had no idea. Did these people ever stop? She felt exhausted watching them. How was she to learn more if no one spoke to her?

She decided to be brazen. At least that would catch their attention. If nothing else, it would invite punishment. Something would happen. Anything was better than just standing there.

She watched a maid slice fresh bread and turn away from it to pick up a tray. Mira walked straight up to the counter and took a slice. She closed her eyes and bit into it. It was delicious, still warm and soft on the inside. "Best bread I've ever tasted", she thought. She hadn't realised how hungry she was. But she was jerked out of her reverie with a sudden awareness of something odd going on around her. She opened her eyes and at first she couldn't tell what was different. But then she realised that all motion and noise in the kitchen had stopped completely. There was an eerie silence, a deadly silence. Everyone had stopped whatever they had been doing, some still in mid-motion, hands, knives, trays hanging in mid air. All activity had come to a complete halt. They were staring at her in shocked disbelief, mouths and eyes wide open. No one moved or said a word. It felt to Mira like they'd actually stopped breathing. She took another bite putting on the mask of a rebel, feeling stronger in her determination. Still no one moved. Not even a twitch.

She took a third bite. She no longer noticed her hunger or the taste of the bread. Her curiosity had peaked. What were they going to do? Someone sighed, picked up the cup she had let drop onto the counter, slowly turned around and went back to her work, although it seemed to Mira with far less energy, her body drooping under some heavy new weight she had acquired . Gradually a few others followed suit. But a very young looking maid standing not far from where Mira was kept staring on. Mira noticed how emaciated she looked and guessed she was starving. She dared not offer her bread, fearing the girl would not be able to resist. It was fine for her to face punishment. All she needed to do if things went too far was to wish herself back home, but she couldn't lead another person into a trap. So she abruptly dropped the rest of the slice down on the counter, still watching the girl.

The girl had tears in her eyes. It took a huge effort for her to wrench herself away from the temptation. But wrench herself she did. With painful movements she turned away and did her best to get back to work.

All of this had happened quickly. Only a few minutes had passed since Mira had picked up the bread, and yet already the door was kicked open. They were fast. Two large, strongly built men walked straight up to her and without a word each grabbed her by an arm and took her away. They had purpose and her feet didn't even touch the ground as they hauled her off.

She was carried down a few flights of stairs. They unlocked a metal door and then re-locked it after they went through. Followed by more steps down until they pretty much threw her out of their grasp. She found herself flung on cold stone floor in what could have been a dark cave.

It took her eyes a while to adjust to the dark. There was not much to see it turned out. She was in a dark, damp, cold basement. She could not see the edges, so she assumed it couldn't have been too small.

The place had been quiet when she entered, but gradually she heard sounds start up in the dark; breathing, sobs,… They had probably been stunned into silence when the door had opened, waiting in fear and dread, and now that they knew it was only another poor prisoner, they went back to their grieving and pain.

Mira felt like she could not bear any more. She wanted to reach out to them, hold them, comfort them. At the same time she wanted to shake them awake. All this suffering, by so many people. Surely they could defeat an army of any size, no matter with how many weapons through sheer strength in numbers. Even if they simply went on strike and refused to work, the great businesses and households would come to a standstill. What did they have to lose anyway? They were all dying. And not only that, but they were suffering every step of the way. This was unbearable, inhuman. Why not make one last stand?

But, it seemed, their souls had been beaten out of them and any action, even the strength to stand by a decision of inaction, was beyond their reach. As long as there's hope, people struggle on and are capable of bending their will to any strong wind. Funny how hope can give the power to fight or endure in any way available.

Her heart ached. She felt exasperated. But there was nothing she could do. "It's all imaginary anyway" she told herself. The words rang hollow. At that moment it all felt way too real.

"I've had enough" she said, out loud without realising, "take me back Pixie"

She was relieved to find herself back in her usual world, but her feelings of distress, frustration, confusion and anger stayed with her.

Taking a step out of the intensity of a situation and looking at it from a distance creates objective clarity and helps us unravel our emotional responses and habitual ways of seeing from the basic truth of the situation. Only in this state can we make clear, wise, objective decisions.

We can always step back and out of the intensity of the situation by simply taking a few deep breaths, becoming calmer, watching with curiosity, becoming more aware. A conscious separation of self from what's happening around and inside, from words, thoughts and feelings and we're there. Peace inside and clearer vision…

Mira had her question ready as soon as Pixie appeared: "Can you take me back to when it all began? I can't understand how this could have happened. How could a whole society allow itself to be destroyed like that?"

Pixie looked like she had been expecting Mira's request. "Are you ready?"

"Yes" Mira closed her eyes.

A quick flash and Mira knew she had arrived. She opened her eyes. She was sitting in a very busy cafe. A hot cup of coffee was placed on the table she was seated at. She looked around. It was definitely meant for her and she was grateful. She needed the coffee to give her courage and energy. She was determined to do whatever it took for her to understand what had happened this time. She would not wish herself away prematurely come what may. She felt her body brace itself for the experience. She had to understand, because just maybe that would help her find a way of preventing such a disaster from happening in her own world. Her society was moving in a similar direction after all.

The people around her were dressed normally. No one was in rags and Mira saw no obvious display of poverty or distress in her immediate surroundings. An animated conversation was taking place at the table closest to hers. She studied the faces of the group sitting in conversation. Amongst them, she recognised the man she had spoken to on the streets. He looked much younger and his eyes had not yet lost their spark. He was talking loudly, his face animated, his cheeks flushed, his eyes blazing. He was excited and mid speech when Mira started to listen in. The others were listening, shaking their heads, nodding, but not saying much. Mira concentrated on his words.

"I tell you. This can't continue. We need to do something. I say you run the article John. You're good at stirring up emotions. That article you wrote about the government's anti-immigration stance was amazing. Remember all the messages of support that came flooding in afterwards? You got people thinking and more importantly, feeling. For a time people were ready to revolt. You aroused their concern. You created a sense of community and resolve"

"Yes, but I also aroused the government's interest. Don't you remember them confiscate all my papers and my computer? They did not hesitate to threaten either. They made it very clear that if I ever write something like that again, my papers would not be the only things taken away."

"They let you go though. It's not as if you suffered. There's still such a thing as free speech in this country you know and human rights, of sorts, at least officially there is"

"My wife certainly didn't appreciate our house being searched top to bottom. And neither did I for that matter. All that distress. And for what? A few lousy messages. People got excited and ranted along with me for a while, all the while staying anonymous, taking no risks for themselves and then slowly everything went quiet, as it always does. They went back to their comfortable lives, but I'm still being watched. Nothing has changed. All those people you refer to did nothing and quickly forgot, while I'm still blacklisted. My wife still wakes up in fear in the middle of the night and our relationship has been strained ever since. She never forgave me. As far as she is concerned, it was selfish of me, what I did. Family comes first, she says and safety and our standard of living are much more important than throwing my opinions around. Let each take care of themselves. She says, where were your so-called friends when the authorities harassed you and took our things away. And she's right. Michael, back me up here" he looked at the other man seated at their table and received acknowledgement with a nod.

"But we can't just sit around and do nothing"

"Well, you do something then. I've tried. People talk, but when it comes to action, either they lack courage, or they don't care enough. They have their own day to day worries to deal with. Unemployment is increasing, lives are getting tougher. They have families to take care of. No one wants to be blacklisted. No one wants their phones and emails tapped. You don't want that either, in spite of all your big talk"

"Of course not, but I would do it if I could. I don't have your knack at words though. What I write wouldn't create any interest at all"

"You're good at talking"

"No one listens" At this he looked down at his drink.

The third man, Michael spoke. The mood was becoming gloomy at the table "Look, what they are doing might not seem right to us. We don't like it, but it's what the people want. It's true we have a problem with immigration. And who knows, maybe we need tougher rules. This government has been voted in by the people we say we're trying to protect twice in a row now. We might not agree with them, but it is a democracy after all and we have to respect what the majority vote for. Unfortunately we're all having to suffer the consequences"

The first man glared at him. "Lack of vision, lack of understanding, no ability to think, insufficient education. They gulp down whatever propaganda is sent their way, broken down into tasty looking bite size morsels to make it easy for them to swallow the whole garbage. Their emotions raised, nationalism waved around like a flag pointing at a treasure. People don't know what they're doing."

"Nonsense. You don't believe that any more than I do"

"Well, the government's anti-immigration policy is getting them a lot of votes. In fact it's the driving topic of politics at the moment and they are popular for it. They are hardly going to change course because of a lousy article"

"That's not the only problem. The economy is collapsing. Money's wasted every day and health and education and social care are suffering. We pay more, they give less. It's a mess. The gap between the rich and the poor is increasing. Unemployment, homelessness are both out of control. People are angry and depressed and most don't even know why. It's all doom and gloom. The news is full of repetitive bad news. We're destroying ourselves and we don't want to know."

Michael glanced at his watch "I have to go" he said and got up. John left with him. Mira saw her chance. She practically wanted to start the conversation with, do you remember me? But of course, that would have made no sense to her new, old friend.

She leaned over towards his table and said "Excuse me, sorry, I couldn't help overhear some of your conversation. Can I join your table?" He shrugged. "I agree something needs to be done, but have no idea what could be done" she added, hoping it would serve as an opening for him to start talking again.

She joined his table and his silence. But he was a natural talker and his silence did not last long.

"The problem is, no one knows what to do, and no one really cares either"

Mira had nothing to say to this.

"Least of all the politicians. All they care about is their positions, their pockets, their comforts, holding onto power. All short-sighted, ego driven, selfish, every last one of them. The irony is, as much as I hate the current government, there's no alternative. The others are just as bad, perhaps worse. What does it really matter? I should just walk away, live in peace in my little space. Maybe move to a different country."

He continued after another short silence "What *is* the alternative? They're all as bad as each other. We need someone who has strong morals, a conscience, one who cares enough to take a stand and is not driven solely by his selfish ambitions"

"Why don't you?"

"Who would listen to me? I'm controversial so I can catch the attention of a small group for a short while, but I don't have what they call charisma, no one would follow me, not in large enough numbers for sure. And anyway, I have no answers either. I don't know how to fix any of this mess. More money for departments that need it, for the health services, for schools, for social care and police. But it's not just the money. They're increasing their grip on free speech without anyone realising. They use terrorism as an excuse to watch and control everyone and people let them, believing it's in their interest, for their safety the government says. Where will this all end? It can't be good"

No, it can't and won't be, Mira thought. But she had no more answers than he did. She had no idea how they could stop the free fall they had initiated into the abyss. They had started a downward spiral, which was gathering up momentum each day. In fact her mind had gone blank. She had to remind herself that she was there to watch and learn, not to change their future or fix their problems. But a quiet thought had already entered her mind: why not? What better way to learn and experience than to be a part of it? She wondered if that were possible. Something in her suggested it was. After all, she could do whatever she wanted to, couldn't she?

"We could start by gathering people who do care. Different people, with different opinions, a variety of knowledge and experience. So the group covers the views of a large section of society and is based on communication, honesty and intelligent compromise. We start by talking. I'm sure with some thought we'll come up with something. Some way to improve the situation. Maybe it will take a few wrong starts and turns, but the one thing we can't afford to do is nothing"

"I agree, but the cost can be great. A strong anti-government article and my friend's house was searched, his stuff confiscated and examined. He is continuously watched and listened to. He spent a night in jail. His experience has shut him up for good. They're heavy handed. And he's right. Nothing changed in spite of his efforts and suffering"

"So you're going to give up?"

He sighed and another heavy silence followed.

Mira decided to leave it at that, at least for the moment. She wished him a nice day and left. He barely noticed. She walked out of the cafe. Her surroundings were familiar. Not exactly the same as the world she had just left, but similar enough to recognise it for what it was. The resemblance was too striking for her to ignore. She pondered on the situation at home. Yes, there were too many similarities to brush off. Ego driven, corrupt politicians and people too busy with their daily lives to take much notice as everything went from bad to worse. Anger and resentment at 'others' as unemployment and poverty increased. It was an all too familiar story.

With no other plan in mind, she kept roaming the streets, her mind full of questions and thoughts.

"Politics is beyond me" she thought, "it's not my place, or role to be part of it, nor does it hold any interest for me". But wasn't it exactly this type of thinking that had gotten this world into the fix it would find itself a few decades down the line?

She felt exhausted. What could one person do? Nothing much she decided. She needed to talk to Pixie. At least she could ask Pixie her questions more openly, and get some answers she was helplessly groping around to find.

Pixie didn't physically appear before her, but Mira was sure she could feel her presence.

"What shall I do Pixie?"

"You don't need to do anything honey. You're here to learn. Then again, you can do whatever you like to. Learn through experience if you can, become a part of it if you like. Whatever you do, whatever route you choose, you will still learn as long as you remain open to everything and don't get caught up in it at a personal, emotional level. Stay detached, as an observer, even as an active observer if that's what you choose to do. But remember, your involvement must stay as an outsider's. That will help keep you clear and objective."

"You could say that about real life Pixie. If we're open to it, we learn from every single event and experience. And yet, there's still always a better way and a worse one, the right path and…" she was going to say wrong path, but at least in her mind she knew there was no such thing. Not really. As long as she learned and changed with her experiences they were all gifts. "Is that my lesson Pixie? Act in the way you feel is best and most beneficial for all, then go with the flow, act and re-act, learn and change day by day, moment by moment?"

"Perhaps"

"I can see their dilemma. How can they act when they have so much to lose? They don't know that non-action will result in a far worse future for all of them. And they're caught up in their daily lives anyway. There's not much space to look up and think about the bigger picture. I expect I'd be the same if I was living in this world"

"In a way you are. You noticed the similarities. And the same can be said for any world. There's always much that can be changed for the better. And there's always too much that absorbs a person's immediate attention. Duties, desires. You get caught up in a world that ends up driving and controlling you, when all of you should take a step back, stand above it, separate from it so you can see clearly and then you can control and drive your own world rather than being dragged any old way by it. You take the detail too seriously, get lost in the minutiae and lose the bigger picture and forget who you are"

"I think I need to take a break Pixie. It's time to go back. I could always come back if I wanted to, couldn't I?"

"Yes, you could. But you don't need to go anywhere to see these things happen. These are events of your time, of your world. And the attitudes are those of people everywhere.

There's something beyond all of this Mira and that's what you need to experience and reach for"

"Okay" she said, her voice resigned. She was too tired to think, so she let it go.

She found herself back in her bedroom and threw herself on her bed, still dressed, but too exhausted to do anything other than collapse.

In spite of her tiredness, her sleep was broken, interrupted by dreams and images. She tossed and turned all night, unable to settle or get enough rest. Deformed people entered her dreams, turning them into nightmares. They were snarling at her, or screaming in pain. Their faces engraved with lines of suffering. Nothing but rags covering their emaciated bodies.

It was still pitch black when she woke up with a start. The last image was vivid in her mind. A woman had been screaming at her. One eye swollen and nothing but skin where the other eye should have been, as if the eye had been sealed shut and the skin smoothed over so that no sign an eye had once been there and seen out of remained. Her nose was large and crooked. Her mouth lop-sided and open wide mid scream. There was a viciousness about her that haunted Mira even now that she was awake.

She sat up in bed, too disturbed to lie down, too tired to get up. She watched her breath, trying very hard to let go of the image and fill her mind with nothing but her breathing instead. Her thoughts kept going back to her dreams, but she willed herself to return to her breathing again and again. She knew she would not be able to make sense of any of it, caught up as she was in the distress of the images.

Gradually and eventually, after what felt to her like an infinity, her mind did settle and she was able to lie back down. She kept her focus on her breath, until gradually the unconsciousness of deep sleep took over.

Life is a journey, made up of many journeys combined. Each journey starts with the first step, eventually reaching its peak. But to get there, we must first take the first step.

Stay open to where the path may take you and what you might encounter along the way. Accept whatever life offers with gratitude. Follow its guidance with a light heart and a smile on your face.

She still felt unsettled when she woke up. Her heart was beating fast and her chest felt tight. She got up slowly. She felt at a loss mentally, but she knew that didn't really matter. Her life had been turned upside down in recent days and she felt too listless and powerless to want to try to pull herself together. Things would take their own course and she would drift along with them. She wasn't sure anything really mattered anymore. She was overcome by a sense of life's futility and senselessness. Her main feeling was one of distress faced with what she perceived to be the pointlessness of it all and the impending doom the world was hurling itself towards.

She was gazing thoughtlessly out of the window when Pixie appeared.

"I don't feel up for much Pixie. I feel empty and low"

"I'd be worried if you didn't feel that way after your previous experience. It's natural and human. Who said you should not feel distress? Feeling things is a human concept. It's universal and natural. What differentiates people from each other is what they do with their emotions. Responses are what matter and what you have control over. Emotions are what you become aware of and accept. Come now, don't look so forlorn, what would you prefer? To live like a robot?"

"No, of course not. But I wish I knew what to do, what the right course of action is."

"Maybe it's time now to take you somewhere else. Some place where things are very different indeed. I think you'll like it"

Mira didn't answer. At that moment she was sure anything would be better than the reality playing out in her head.

"What is reality?" she heard Pixie say.

"Is this not real?" she asked waving her arm around her, taking in her surroundings. "Am I not real? Is what I feel right now not real?"

"Is it? Perhaps that depends on your point of view and your definition of what real is"

Mira did not understand, but she did not feel up to arguing with Pixie and a helpful question did not come to her mind either.

"Don't worry. You'll understand"

"So where to next?"

"Are you ready?"

"No, I don't want to do anything at all at the moment. But then, anything would be better than nothing. I can't stay like this. It's as if the walls, in fact the very sky, are closing in on me. My thoughts are eating me up. "

"I think you're ready" Pixie said and Mira closed her eyes.

Mira opened her eyes in fresh air. She gazed down at a vast ocean, water as far as she could see. She was sitting on grass on the side of a mountain, not too high up, surrounded by trees and wild flowers. A soft breeze ran through her hair. The sight that met her eyes was dramatic and beautiful. A sense of serenity spread through her. She didn't want to move in case even a little rustle disturbed the magic.

She stayed where she was for a while, enjoying the scene, the breeze, the ocean air and mighty roar of the waves. She felt like she could stay there, utterly still, forever. But doing nothing was against her nature. After a while her attention searched for a diversion, she was feeling restless. When nothing offered itself to her, she knew she had to move.

She got up slowly and looked around her. Behind her stood a small cluster of huts. They had large roofs extending beyond the walls they were placed on by a large margin, sloping down towards the earth. Plants and trees she did not recognise were growing tall all around her. Their colours were so vibrant, she felt like her eyes could not possibly take in all that richness.

"Soul food", she thought.

Birds sang in a nearby tree and apart from the breeze, ocean and birds, she heard nothing. She walked towards the huts slowly, at peace inwardly and curious. Soft conversations and the sounds of pots being used became audible in the distance and she started to move towards the source of these sounds. She found her way between some huts towards the back of the cluster where she saw a structure with the same kind of roof, only larger, and built onto trees instead of walls. This one was open on all four sides, it had no walls. There was a large fire in the centre and all kinds of cooking equipment were scattered around it. It was a simple structure, and in such warm weather Mira could see no reason to build walls. It was so much nicer to be undivided from those beautiful surroundings. "How perfect" she thought.

She saw a handful of people squatting under the roof, cleaning pots and utensils. She moved towards them. One of them looked up and smiled. As she approached, another one stopped what he was doing and came out to greet her.

"Welcome" he said. "Were we hard to find?"

"No" Mira replied.

"We have just eaten, but we can prepare you something if you're hungry"

"No, thank you, there's no need"

"Make yourself comfortable"

She sat down to one side and leaned against a tree. She was in no hurry to move, or speak. She watched the others as they continued with their work, cleaning and tidying away pots, pans, bowls. They worked at a comfortable pace. They did not seem to be in any hurry.

When they were done, the man who had welcomed her came towards her and asked "Would you like to join us in meditation?"

Mira nodded. She followed him and noticed the others were following in silence close behind. They walked out towards the edge of the clearing and sat in a semi-circle facing the ocean. Mira sat next to the leader when he motioned her to do so. They sat cross-legged and closed their eyes. Outwardly she did exactly what she observed the others do, but inwardly she had no idea what she ought to do next. Everyone was quiet. They looked so peaceful, their spines erect, a gentle smile lingering on their lips, their shoulders relaxed. Their faces shone with an expression of serenity and quiet joy. She sat quietly listening to the ocean and the birds and gazing over the faces in the gathering from time to time.

Gradually her limbs began to ache. It was hard sitting tall and still for so long. Her legs had gone numb and her shoulders were hurting. She started to feel bored. She so wanted to get up and stretch her limbs out, to move in any way she could. She would have happily lied down on the spot. But the others were so still and quiet, she was afraid to disturb them or make an embarrassing spectacle of herself. So she forced herself to stay still.

After more time, Mira had no idea how long, it could have been minutes crawling by like hours, or actual hours beating up her aching muscles, she could not stand it anymore. They looked like they might stay like that forever. She very carefully, quietly extended her arms up and stretched. No one moved, so she stretched out her legs too. Still nothing from the others, so she carefully lay down on the spot and closed her eyes.

She must have fallen asleep. The sun was already very low over the ocean when she opened them again. The group was no longer there. Just as she started to wonder what she ought to do and whether she should even stay, having shown herself to be such an unworthy guest, she saw someone approach her. She got up to her feet and was just about to apologise, but the woman who had come to fetch her spoke first "come join us. You must be hungry"

She followed the woman back to the wall-less structure, where she found a small group of people sitting under the roof in a circle. As she approached them, she saw another woman serving out some lumpy, thick meal into bowls, which was then passed hand to hand to the opposite side of the circle, the next bowl stopped at the person nearer and so it continued, until they all had a bowl in their hands. They had left a space for her in the circle. As she moved towards it the woman serving held out a bowl for her too. She sat down and saw a spoon lying on the ground in front of her. She hesitated to pick the spoon up, no one else had. They were holding their bowls with both hands and had closed their eyes. She did the same.

A voice, deep and gentle, started to speak. She did not understand what he said, but guessed it was a prayer of sorts. When he stopped speaking there was a moment's silence, then they started to eat.

Their movements were full of ease and grace. No sign of impatience, hurry or distraction disturbed the gathering. They did not speak. They seemed to taste and enjoy each mouthful, slowly. The sludge in her bowl tasted far better than she had expected it to. It was dark brown in colour and could have passed for a type of oatmeal. It didn't taste like anything else she had tried before.

She realised she was very hungry, and although what she ate did not look like much to her eyes, her stomach was satisfied, though not completely full even after she'd finished.

Once they were all done eating, the bowls and spoons were gathered up and taken over to a corner to be washed. She wanted to help, but everyone else knew where they fit in while she did not and she felt too timid to step in. A woman must have guessed her confusion. She came up to her and quietly said: "You are tired. Tonight you rest. Tomorrow you can help. Come with me"

Mira followed her to a hut. There was not much inside, a simple low bed, and a few other belongings, but Mira did not look around. She was led to the bed, where she lay down and fell asleep straight away.

She woke up at dawn, feeling refreshed, fully awake and full of energy. There was a mad chorus of hundreds of birds welcoming the rising sun as it took its time moving slowly into view. The hut walls were washed in a soft, gentle pre-dawn light. She looked around. Apart from the bed, there were only a few shelves on one wall and a hearth. She was in no hurry to get up. She enjoyed listening to the bird songs and the quiet serenity of the place for a while.

As the sun made its increasingly dazzling ascent in the sky, Mira got up and walked outside. There was no sign of anyone else around. She walked out towards the ocean and that's where she saw them. They were sitting in a half circle, facing the ocean, as they had done the day before, spines erect, faces serene, eyes closed. She sat a short distance away wondering at these peaceful people. She gazed out at the ocean lost in thought.

The ocean was fully awake too and was roaring up into huge waves. She could see the water rise up, like the full neck of a snake, linger for a moment once lifted, a dark cave hovering above the vast body of ocean. Then starting from one end, the wave started to crash down, creating bright white foam, the crash moving its way all the way down the wave until it had all turned into a mighty white beast which came roaring all the way into land. A continuous dance of water, foam and waves. It was mesmerising. She wondered at the sheer power each wave held within it, the way it rose up to its peak in a blasting crescendo and then came crashing back down to join the ocean once more.

The group sat as they were for hours. As she was not too near them, Mira felt free to move as she liked and time passed by more easily. They got up eventually and went their separate ways, off to do Mira knew not what.

One of them, the one that had welcomed her the day before, walked up to her. "Why are you here?" he asked.

At first she was baffled. The question had caught her by surprise. Here by the ocean? Here with them? She decided there was no need for a long explanation. "To learn" she replied.

He smiled and sat down beside her. They sat in silence enjoying the ocean and the breeze that had started up.

"It takes a lot of patience and quite a lot of effort too." He said eventually.

"I want to try" Mira responded. She had been brought here for a reason. She loved the place and her whole being had been filled with calm since she had arrived. Besides, she was curious. She wanted to learn their meditation, she assumed that was what they were doing. She wanted to learn how to be able to sit still so peacefully for long hours on end. She wanted to learn how to find that serenity within herself and the joy exuding through their gentle smiles. And besides, she did not yet want to leave this heavenly place. Most of all, she loved being by the ocean, surrounded by its voice, sight and energy.

"There's a school not far from here. One of us will take you there later today"

Mira had assumed they would teach her and that she would stay in this wonderful place. She was disappointed. He must have sensed that, because he added "We are here to practise, we cannot teach you. The school is very good. People come from all over to learn at it. When you're ready you're welcome to come back here and join us, if that is still what you want"

Mira knew that was the end of the conversation. She did not feel inclined to go to any school. It reminded her of childhood. That was not the kind of learning she had had in mind. "I can leave whenever I want", she reminded herself and decided to at least see the school and give it a go. She nodded.

He smiled and left her side.

Mira spent the next few hours watching the ocean, wandering around and touching and smelling the flowers and trees. She did not think she had ever seen a place this beautiful in her life.

But the time came for her to leave eventually and she dutifully followed her assigned guide.

They walked inland following a very narrow path. The path then started to turn back out. Eventually they were walking up a steep path, the mountain rising up one side of them and cliffs dropping down to the ocean on their other side. They continued to walk in silence for a very long time. Mira was feeling tired, her legs started to ache, but she made an effort and kept up with her guide. He seemed to be completely at ease, not strained by the incline or the roughness of the path in any way, not showing any signs of fatigue.

Just as Mira started to think she truly could not walk any longer they turned a bend and there in front of her the path opened up into a huge clearing. They made their way onwards and in the near distance rooftops started to appear. As they approached, she saw a cluster of structures, different shapes and sizes, surrounded by trees and small meadows. She could see farmland to her left and people working, walking, spread out all over the place.

Her guide led her right up to a small hut and walked inside. She followed. It was empty. They sat down on the ground and started to wait. She wondered why he didn't go out and find whoever they were waiting for. She was tired, hungry and feeling increasingly irritated.

They did not wait for long however. Shortly a woman entered the hut. She and her guide exchanged a few words of greeting and he left.

The woman looked Mira up and down. Her face was welcoming, although Mira could imagine her being very strict if necessary.

"Welcome" she said. "I'll show you around first, then we can go through the schedule and you can start straight away"

Mira wanted to say she was tired and hungry, but she simply nodded.

The spiritual path is not easy and the practise of meditation takes perseverance and patience. Trust your heart, your teachers and guides. Their actions, their very way of being speak louder than words.

"Once seated, strive to still your thoughts. Make your mind one-pointed in meditation, and your heart will be purified." Krishna to Arjuna in the Bhagavad Gita, VI: 12-13, translation by Eknath Easwaran

"Through constant effort they learn to withdraw the mind from selfish cravings and absorb it in the Self. Thus they attain the state of union." Krishna to Arjuna in the Bhagavad Gita, VI: 15, translation by Eknath Easwaran

"The practise of meditation frees one from all affliction. This is the path of yoga. Follow it with determination and sustained enthusiasm. Renouncing wholeheartedly all selfish desires and expectations, use your will to control the senses. Little by little, the mind will become stilled in the Self. Wherever the mind wanders, restless and diffuse in its search for satisfaction without, lead it within; train it to rest in the Self." Krishna to Arjuna in the Bhagavad Gita, VI: 23-26, translation by Eknath Easwaran

The name of her host was Maria. She was a cheerful woman and spent time with Mira, pointing out the various parts of the ashram. Classes were held in a wall-less structure, covered by a large roof, similar to the one her previous hosts had prepared and eaten their food under, although it was much larger. There were a few buildings that housed the students and staff, there was a place for eating, with a simple kitchen to one side. And to Mira's delight, there were numerous gardens scattered all around.

Tranquillity seeped from every corner. No one paid them much attention as they wandered around. Once out from among the little buildings, they came to edge of the ashram, where she could look down onto the ocean. They were very high up. And there, near the edge of the clearing, she saw quite a large gathering of people, all seated facing the ocean, eyes closed, deep in meditation. They were covered with another roof structure built on to the trees. Here Maria became very quiet and only pointed.

She then took Mira into one of the buildings which had rows of low beds in it. They walked up to one of them and Maria told Mira it was hers. Mira counted the beds from the door, as that was the only way she could distinguish it from the others when she returned.

"We start at three in the morning" Maria said. "You saw where we meditate. That's where you need to go first thing. Breakfast is at six. Classes start at half past seven. You won't have time to be bored here. Lunch is eaten at twelve thirty, after which we all take care of our duties. You will do your part as we take turns farming, cleaning the ashram and preparing food. None of it is especially hard work. Do it all with an attitude of joy and love in your heart. In the afternoon at three, there are some more classes and the day ends with meditation. We finish at seven thirty. I expect you'll be ready to sleep by then. If not, you can meditate for as long as you want. Don't forget the early start though."

Mira took it all in. A long day of study and meditation. She expected that the performance of her duties would be a welcome diversion from all the sitting and listening.

"You're too late to join meditation now and I expect you're tired. Enjoy some free time, you won't have much of it from tomorrow, and rest. Do you have any questions?"

Mira had none. But just as Maria was about to walk away, she asked "what time is it?"

Maria glanced up towards the sky. "Around six. You can go to bed early tonight if you like"

Mira was exhausted and it must have shown. She thanked Maria and slowly made her way back to her bed. She was asleep within moments.

She woke up to the sound of movement all around her. It was still dark, but people were getting ready quietly. She followed them out of the building and saw buckets of water standing over to one side. They each took turns dipping a bowl into a bucket and washing their face. Mira did the same and followed them out to the meditation area. She sat down amongst them, adjusting her seat to make herself as comfortable and erect as possible. She watched as they settled and closed their eyes.

She did not know how to meditate, so she let her mind drift. She liked the place and decided she would stay for a while, at least a day or two. The schedule seemed a little harsh, but maybe she'd find it interesting. And with that thought, already, boredom started to creep in as she sat. She really was not at all used to being still. She was feeling fidgety and increasingly uncomfortable. She wanted so badly to get up and stretch out her aching limbs. After a while the wait became unbearable. She was tempted to wish herself home, but something held her back. The minutes passed by painfully slowly. She reached a point when she desperately wanted to scream and shout. She could not stand it anymore. How could these people remain so still for so long? She started moving her limbs, as quietly as she could. But she had reached the point where she no longer cared about disturbing anyone or being told off. No one seemed to notice though, so she got up and walked away.

She wandered round the gardens until she heard the sound of people walking and talking quietly. Ready to face whatever might come she joined them, but no one said anything, or even looked at her in any particular way. She joined them for breakfast. A similar sludge to the one she had been given on her first day in this world was served, but this time she found the taste very bland. She felt even more irritation rise up in her. Why was she eating this shit? What was she doing here?

Once more she had an overwhelming desire to leave and still something held her back. Probably because it would have felt too much like failure. "I hate it here", she thought and was surprised at herself. She changed her thoughts to it's hard instead. That felt less harsh. She decided that staying here in itself was a challenge, which made her even more determined to stay.

Just as they were finishing, a man approached her from behind. "Let's have a chat" he said. "Here we go", Mira thought," I'm going to be told off as if I were a five year old". The man led her to one of the gardens and they sat down.

"It's hard at first" he said gently. There was no indication of severity or anger in his voice. No, Mira was not going to be told off after all. "You get used to it. Your body adjusts and you are able to sit with increasing comfort. Your mind gets trained and gradually you feel less bored, or irritated, or angry. But it takes time. Sometimes a long time. And diligence. Do your best. Don't get angry with yourself. Know that we have all been through your experience and you do find more and more peace inside of you as you continue. We're here to help and support each other through the process and through all that inevitably comes up when we have time, space and quiet for them to. It's never easy facing our demons and having nowhere to run away from them. Just keep trying."

"I couldn't stay" Mira stated simply, referring to her leaving meditation practise mid-way.

"That's okay. When you can't sit any more, if nothing you try helps, then you need to get up and leave. But please do so quietly so as not to disturb the others. Avoid beating yourself up about it and getting angry with yourself. That just makes things worse. It does get easier I promise, and more pleasant"

Mira had no doubt in the truth of the man's words and was glad to hear she could get up when she needed to.

"I don't know how to meditate" she said.

"You'll be instructed" was his simple answer.

At first Mira understood very little of what she was taught. There were too many terms and words that were unfamiliar to her. In fact the whole subject was new to her. By the end of each day, she was exhausted, her brain melting from trying so hard to concentrate, listen and think.

Her first meditation instruction was given on her second day there. Directly after breakfast she was approached by a man who motioned to her to follow him. They sat down cross-legged across from each other in one of the gardens.

"How are you getting on with your meditation?"

"I'm not. I don't know how to meditate and when I try to sit still, I can't. I can't even still my mind. I get frustrated and impatient and fidgety. To be honest, I'm finding it torturous"

He smiled. "You'll get used to it. It gets easier. Let's give it a go, shall we?"

She nodded.

His first instruction was, "Sit straight"

Mira obeyed.

"Close your eyes. Take your attention to your breath. Just allow yourself to breathe comfortably. Don't control it, or force it. Be gentle. Stay relaxed. Now focus on your breath. Try and let go of all other thoughts. Watch your breath"

Mira tried for a few minutes. It was hard to relax with the man watching her. And although she was aware of her breath, which was racing, her mind was still busy, running after all kind of thoughts. It would not do as she bid it to. The harder she tried to focus, the more frustrated she felt and the more her mind rebelled.

"You're trying too forcefully. Just relax. It's normal for the mind to wander, that's its nature. Don't expect it to suddenly stop at your bidding. There's no point getting angry with it, that's counterproductive. Just keep bringing it back to your breath from wherever it goes whenever you noticed it's wandered off again, without anger, without judgement, without irritation. That is the practise. The mind wanders off and we bring it back, again and again and again. Patiently. Gently."

Mira tried. She sighed. She ordered her mind to be still, but instead it seemed to rise up even more, practically pushing her up and away with it. She fought and remained still, her mind started to shout. She wanted to cry out, 'enough', to her mind, to her instructor, it didn't even matter, just shout and run.

"I can't"

"But you already are."

"My mind is too busy and rebellious"

"Okay. Let's try to focus it on something more tangible. Start counting your breath. Count to four as you inhale and four as you exhale. Rhythmic, steady counts. Focus on the counts, feeling your breath at the same time"

Mira found this easier. It gave her mind something to do, something more concrete to focus on. Gradually she settled.

He noticed the change and said "I think this is a good start for you. When we sit for meditation, this is your practise for the next few days. Don't get annoyed, frustrated or angry when you can't focus. You'll find some days are better than others, but your mind will keep wandering. You'll find thousands of thoughts lifting their heads, clamouring for your attention. Accept that, let them go without anger and come back to your breath and the counting. The mind is just like any other muscle in the body. The more you train it, the stronger it's ability to concentrate and be still becomes. Focusing will get easier if you stick with it"

"It's not very relaxing" Mira remarked.

"It is, eventually. All those thoughts are tiring. You are resting your mind when you focus this way. And your attitude during your practise should always be relaxed acceptance and watchfulness. Stressing and straining yourself will only bring up negative emotions. And they'll pull you down the path of further emotions and thoughts, distracting you even further. Accept that this is your mind's nature and you're taming it, day by day, minute by minute. It does get easier. Once you become more comfortable in your practise, you'll find it brings you a deeper joy than anything else you have previously experienced"

It was hard for Mira to imagine reaching that stage, but she decided to take his word for it. After all, they all seemed to have managed to here. She had had plenty of opportunity during what seemed to her utterly fruitless attempts at being still to observe the faces of the others. They all looked so blissfully calm. Most had a soft, smiling expression on their faces and she envied their state of mind.

"I will try"

"Great. That is the best any of us can expect to do at any given time."

She did try, but she continued to find meditation difficult and a calm, empty, serene mind elusive. Sometimes she thought that sitting still for hours on end, not 'doing' anything would drive her absolutely mad. She got irritated and impatient often. As time passed though, some days, a deep peace would settle on her and it all became worth the effort, even if only for a few minutes.

The setting was spectacular and when she did have some spare time, walking along the cliffs gave her immense joy.

She could not have said what kept her there exactly. Some days she felt like a mass of anger and frustration ready to explode. Sometimes her emotions felt so forceful, she thought she might blow up and destroy not only herself, but everything and everyone else around her. And yet she persevered. She kept telling herself, one more day, just one more day, and so the days passed and she held on.

"O Sanjaya, tell me what happened at Kurukshetra, the field of dharma, where my family and the Pandavas gathered to fight." Bhagavad Gita I:1, translation by Eknath Easwaran

There had been excitement among the students the day before, when they had been told the study of the Bhagavad Gita would start the next day. Mira did not know what the Bhagavad Gita was about, but could not help but feel excited and curious with them. The group's energy was infectious.

Her meditation was progressing, she had to admit to herself, although way too slowly for her liking. They really had meant it when they stressed the need for patience and perseverance. Some days were good. She felt peace spread within her, in and through every cell of her body. On days like that the world seemed a heaven, and life, hers and all others' nothing short of a miracle, full of joy and beauty. At moments like these anything was possible, anything could be achieved. Then some other days she simply could not settle and she left meditation in a worse frame of mind than when she had sat down to it, unable to escape her feelings of irritation, anger, frustration and disappointment with herself.

Whenever she tried to get help from one of the teachers, who were always full of understanding and patience towards her and her moods and annoyances, the advice they gave always came down to the same thing: That she should go easier on herself, not be so harsh, not force so much and simply be aware, notice, watch and always pay attention to whatever came up for her and notice the resulting responses.

Was she angry? What did anger feel like? Notice the emotion. How did she know it was anger? What did she feel in her body, in her soul? What was she thinking? What shape and sensation did these thoughts bring with them? How did she want to react and how did she actually react? Keep watching. Same with anything that came up. Frustration? Watch it and the ripples the emotion creates in mind, body and soul. Boredom? Same process. In fact, whatever comes up, no matter how 'good' or 'bad' you might think it is or label it as, understand that it simply is; neither good, nor bad, simply is what it is without labels, nothing more. Accept it as it is, watch it with interest. Notice the constant labelling that goes on in the background, directing your responses, feelings, actions, thoughts. Are you stamping it with 'bad' straight away? Notice that. And the analysing, extending into future possibilities, worrying about things that have not yet happened and may never happen. Is not your frustration a result of one of these labels? A distraction is just a thought, feeling, sensation. Is it not your labelling that turns it into something 'bad'? And from there the feelings of frustration, anger, disappointment are a natural follow-on.

And on and on and on it went. Watch, watch, watch. With interest and acceptance. Taking in every moment as a new experience, without assumptions, expectations, wants, likes, dislikes, frustrations, just as is.

Sometimes she was able to and sometimes the emotion took over and she became a part of it, rather than remaining apart from it and watching it. She felt her whole being fill with the emotion, leading on to thoughts, which then fed the emotion, which in turn fed the thoughts, until she felt trapped in an avalanche of overwhelming feelings. All from a tiny little passing thought that had crept up and fed and been fed.

"You are not your emotions" she had been told. "They are sensations that rise up in you, have a life of their own and when they're done, they die back down. Watch them from afar, don't let them take over you. Notice the physical sensations they create and how these change and pass. Notice how your mind grips onto the emotion, trying to push it away or hold onto it, getting lost in it and the associations created by it, always relating to the past or future, but never to the present, the very moment you are living in."

Someone had told her that when she was in danger of getting carried away by an emotion, she found it helpful to remind herself that she was neither the emotion that came up, nor was the emotion really even a part of her. It was a separate entity that she could either choose to take on, own and make a part of herself, or let go of, in which case it had no option but to pass by, leaving her alone. She had said, "when you feel irritated for example, your natural thought is 'I'm irritated'. Change that around. Instead think 'I'm noticing a sense of irritation in my body or mind or breath. Try and be very specific, noticing the detail, the nuances. So maybe notice that you are feeling it in your chest like a bird's wings fluttering, wanting to take flight. Or whatever it might be. The more you pay attention, the further the distance you place between yourself and whatever has come up for you. It increasingly becomes a distant, separate entity that you no longer need to make a part of you. You become the watcher, the observer, no longer one with the watched or observed. You are then no longer the feeling or sensation, you are separate and it has lost its hold over you. It is us that give them their power over us. We can choose to take that power away by simply letting them go, letting them pass by as if they are not at all important and nothing to do with us."

This advice helped Mira especially. When she thought 'I'm angry', her anger increased until she could bear it no longer. Thoughts of why took over, which became her excuses, which in turn fed the emotion. And there it was, the emotion growing and feeding further similar thoughts, a self feeding, ever growing creature.

But when she managed to separate herself from the feeling of anger, it didn't take over her. And the more she watched it, noticed it, took in the detail, the less she felt it was a part of her at all. Until there was no more anger left to watch, at which point her attention was caught by something else. She truly came to understand how true it was that life and everything in it, from the most dense physical substance, to the least dense emotion or thought is constantly moving, shifting, changing, always and constantly. Everything, physical, mental, emotional, proved itself again and again to be nothing more, nor less, than shifting, changing energy. Some denser and slower, some light and fast. But all forms of energy nonetheless. And as she watched, she saw a fascinating moving screen of life in all its glory, colour and confusion pass through her awareness. The more she was able to stay focused and empty, the slower the images passed her by and the clearer and more distinct they became and the longer the gaps between the images lasted.

Their teacher was talking about the need for each person to review his or her day before going to sleep. This was essentially more practise in increasing awareness; of actions, thoughts and their results, an assessment of the day just lived. He said that was what the first line of the Gita was asking all spiritual aspirants to do. Telling us to constantly look back on our actions, thoughts, feelings and holding them up to the light of objective analysis, objective and non-judgemental. Analysis for the sake of understanding, of getting to know ourselves better, without creating tools for us to beat ourselves up or boost our egos. Compassionate, discriminative, non-judgemental, objective analysis. Only that way can we know who we are and how to further better ourselves. Knowledge brings with it understanding and choices, which mean freedom from habits, tendencies, addictions, unconscious desires, drives, dislikes.

During the inner battle we are all fighting each moment of our lives, the Gita asks us to look at which side has been victorious that day. This battle is ever continuous at more than one level. There is the outward level. How did I act? What did I do? Did I do things for the benefit of others? Did I say or do anything harmful, towards myself or others? Did I act in line with my chosen path or did I not? Was I selfish? Did I fly into a rage? Was I fair? Did I show compassion? The questions we can ask are endless and some will be more pertinent to each of us than others on any given day.

Then there's the internal level. What did I feel throughout the day? When was I angry, resentful, jealous? How did I react to these emotions? Was I driven by my compulsions, acting them out, getting carried away by my desires and dislikes at any time? What were the resulting actions of these emotions and the responses from the outer world? When did I feel compassion, love or peace? How did that work out for me?

And, yet another level is the spiritual level. During my battle to control my mind, to separate myself from my ego, how did I fare? Was I able to focus during meditation, or did my emotions or mental distractions take over?

Mira thought," the answer to that last one is pretty simple for me, I always lose"

She brushed away the thought with a forceful 'be kind to yourself'.

The teacher was still explaining:

"Bhagavad Gita literally means "Song of the Spirit". It is a small section of one of India's great epics, the Mahabharata, the whole of which was created in the form of a spiritual allegory. Within its eighteen chapters, the Gita contains guidance, advice and instructions for all of us, whatever our ambitions, priorities and characters, whatever stage of our spiritual journey we are at, on how to live more fulfilled, happier lives, in line with our true nature. It describes the way, ultimately, to complete freedom, from pain and suffering, from experiencing ups and downs, being tumbled around by the pull of opposites, rebirth and death and being driven beyond our control by our intrinsic drives, likes and dislikes. It holds within its verses the path to leading a spiritual, righteous life and shows us how we can all find inner peace and contentment, no matter what our outer circumstances.

The Gita takes place on the eve of a great battle and is narrated in the form of a dialogue between Arjuna, a warrior king and Lord Krishna, an incarnation of God acting as a charioteer and advisor to Arjuna.

Every word in the Gita, including the names of characters, have symbolic meaning and each verse speaks to us at many different levels. It is possible to read the Gita over and over again throughout our lives and still find within its words new information, new depths of insight and fresh perspectives.

The battle is fought on the holy plain of Kurukshetra, the bodily field of activity. It is the psychological and spiritual battle fought within each and every person every day of our lives, on physical, emotional, mental and spiritual levels.

The battle is fought between the Kurus, our sense and mental tendencies, sons of blind King Dhritarashtra, and the Pandus, our pure, discriminate tendencies. The sense tendencies bring worry, anxiety, illness and ignorance to the bodily kingdom and no matter what stage in our lives we are at, whatever our ambitions and hopes, we all find ourselves fighting these tendencies. While the pure discriminative tendencies bring peace, happiness and health. Hence the battle. If we are to live happy, fulfilled lives our intelligent discriminative tendencies, our soul force must win over our sense driven drives.

The Pandus, five brothers, each represent a different chakra, energy centre, in the body; Yudhishthara the throat chakra, Bhima the heart chakra, Arjuna the solar plexus, Nakula the sacral chakra and Sahadeva the root chakra.

In the Gita, Lord Krishna clearly states the importance of applying the principles of yoga to our everyday lives. His advice and guidance is practical. He suggests and describes different paths we can follow, including the paths of selfless service, devotion, meditation, self-analysis and contemplation. Our choice of path will ultimately depend on our nature, inclinations, tendencies and character and our chosen path might change during the course of our life. We might also choose to follow a combination of several paths. But whichever path we choose to focus on, the Bhagavad Gita is there to light our way and guide us.

Lord Krishna reminds us in Chapter II, verse 40, that no effort made on any spiritual path ever goes to waste, every effort we make is worth our while. He is thereby motivating us to start now in whatever small way we find accessible to us: "On this path effort never goes to waste, and there is no failure. Even a little effort toward spiritual awareness will protect you from the greatest fear." (Translation by Eknath Easwaran)

One of the most important and pertinent verses in the Bhagavad Gita is the very first verse. Dhritarashtra is the blind king, Manas, the ego driven mind and father of a hundred sons, the Kauravas, sense inclinations focused on worldly enjoyment. He is uncle to the Pandus, intelligent discriminative tendencies, sons of Pandu, Buddhi, pure discrimination.

Sanjaya represents impartial introspection and self-analysis and Kurukshetra is the bodily field of activity.

The Gita opens with the value of regular introspection, using our discrimination. It asks us to take a few moments at the end of each day to look back on our activities and thoughts and contemplate on these as objectively as we are able to. How did we fare this day? On the battle field of our physical, mental, emotional and spiritual body which side won? Was it our sense driven impulses or our pure discriminative, intelligent tendencies?

We are not being asked to judge and berate ourselves. We are being asked to train our objective discriminative faculties, to learn to take a step back from and out of our ego led emotional subjective selves and look at our actions to see ourselves more clearly, separate from our blind ego, even if just for a few minutes. We are asked to feel with clear, calm intuition, not with biased, judgemental emotion. As we train ourselves to see our actions and feelings more objectively, we are more able to make intelligent choices in our lives, rather than be driven by our subconscious and unconscious parts, controlled by our likes and dislikes, habits, emotions and belief systems. We take back our right to choose how we act in life's circumstances.

This self-reflection is meant to be at all levels of our being. Physically, what was our behaviour like? How did we act? How did we treat others? What good or bad deeds did we do?

Mentally, how was our thinking? Did we get drawn into negative thought cycles, depression, anger, jealousy, or were we positive, compassionate, loving? Did we succumb to judgement and criticism of ourselves or others? Did we feel resentful or grateful? Did we fall into grief, anger, greed, fear, doubt, pride or were we joyful, forgiving, content, confident, brave and humble?

Spiritually, were we overrun by material, sense driven pursuits, whether in action or thought, or did we follow pure, spiritual lines? If we spent time meditating, did distractions, restlessness or laziness win, or were we able to focus?

Every human being fights on the field of Kurukshetra. Even those who are not interested in spirituality will be fighting this battle, but perhaps on a more material level. We are all, at some level or another striving for happiness and inner peace and trying to win over pain and suffering. The Gita in this verse, as it is throughout, is universal, practical and applicable to each and every one of us at all stages of our lives."

Mira was deeply moved by this verse and its explanation. She understood what had excited the others so much. She felt like an entire new universe had opened itself up to her, with so much to offer and teach and so much joy. She promised herself that even if she succeeded in nothing else, she would at least take this verse to heart and review each day as objectively as she was capble.

The day progressed as usual, Mira was by now used to their routine, their rhythm of studying, learning, meditating, eating, sleeping and the simplicity of her new life. She had become so accustomed to it, her old life felt alien and distant. More often than not, it felt like a story she had read some time long ago. One she knew well, but had never really been part of.

And then there would be moments when it was as if her old life gave her a sharp prick or slap and suddenly she was left wondering what she was doing at the ashram. In those moments she had a wish to leave and go back to her old life.

Not that that life was nicer. But it had loads of distractions. She could avoid being quiet with herself and her emotions and thoughts for days on end. She could live in blissful ignorance. There was always so much to do, to take care of, to worry about. She was more at peace here than she had ever been. But she missed the busyness of that other life. As stressful as all the events could be, as tiring and sometimes boring, she also realised that all the duties and ups and downs of life offered a great distraction from the chaotic life that went on within her. The problem was, even when outer life calmed down, the inner turmoil continued and without the usual distractions she was left with no choice but to face what was continuously going on inside. And that was hard, really hard.

In truth, she had never really managed to stop feeling or dwelling on the multitude of emotions that raged storms in her being. But she could put a safe distance between herself and them by staying busy. Now that she had so much time and space, she found them overwhelming her. Her soul truly was a battle ground, one that was crowded and loud, creating plenty of inner pain in its wake. The inner chaos frustrated and annoyed her, but it fascinated her as well. She realised that although she hardly ever acted out in anger, there was so much of it within her, mostly turned towards herself, darting poisonous arrows into her very being. She wondered where the anger came from. When it appeared, in the moment, it usually appeared out of nowhere, and she felt it must have a source, a root inside her.

She found that all sensations, physical, mental or emotional were like waves. They would rise and roar and tumble forward for a while, disturbing, flushing out and carrying all that lay in their wake, but then eventually they'd crash out or simply wither away. This was true for a pain in a limb, just as much as it was for an emotion, or a state of mind like tiredness. They all came and went if she watched them. In fact they came and went even when she got carried away with them, however then they took longer and created large ripples that lingered on even after they had died out. Sometimes her thoughts fed her emotional turmoil, at times by buying into it, at other times by fighting against it. Either way they held their space, stood their ground and grew stronger and meaner. The only way for them to drift away was if she ignored them, or got distracted by something else, which was really the same as ignoring them.

She struggled with keeping her mind focused, but she kept reminding herself that it was okay that her mind wondered and that too was a part of the process.

Most of all she looked forward to their breaks, when she could walk around, watch the ocean and be free of herself. The ocean drew her to itself constantly. It was hypnotic and strong, cleansing and energising.

Some days she would worry about the world she had left behind. Was time passing by there as it was here? Would she be returning to things as she had left them, or would she find everything changed. She wanted to ask Pixie, but she also did not want to know the answer. If they were moving on, she'd start to worry and want to go back. She could always tell herself that she would return here, but she knew these thoughts and worries were only yet further distractions and she remained resolute on continuing along the path she had started. This felt important to her, more important than anything else ever had.

That night she remembered the day's lesson and before falling asleep she went through her day in her mind. She hadn't done too badly all in all. Her mood had been positive and she had managed to berate herself less. She had done her duties with inner peace and learned as much as she could during class. She had felt a strong sense of gratitude throughout the day, especially for having been brought to this place where she could be introduced to the Bhagavad Gita. Her meditation had been rocky though and she knew she had a long way to go yet until she would be able to sit peacefully, with calm and gentle focus and that gentle smile others held, which mostly still evaded her during meditation.

*"The Self cannot be pierced by weapons or burned by fire;
water cannot wet it, nor can the wind dry it. The Self cannot
be pierced or burned, made wet or dry. It is everlasting and
infinite, standing on the motionless foundations of eternity. The
Self is unmanifested, beyond all thought, beyond all change.
Knowing this, you should not grieve." Krishna speaking
to Arjuna in the Bhagavad Gita II: 23-25, translation by
Eknath Easwaran*

Mira was sitting in a lecture. She was trying to understand
not only in her head, but also in her heart, what their teacher
was saying: "There is the self, that gets involved in all the
emotions. It gets carried away with its desires, its likes and
dislikes, its anger and resentment, and all the other emotions
that we live with and are ruled by. We assume they are a part
of us, but they end up running our lives. Mostly we become
a part of them. Then there is the Self, Atman, that is beyond
the body and the mind, that is unborn and undying, beyond
the array of human emotion. According to Lord Krishna, as
conveyed in the Bhagavad Gita, the wise know themselves to
be this Self and are not affected by the events of the world.
They see the drama of emotions play out in front of them, but
do not get drawn into these. They are able to stay apart from
their experiences, resting in eternal joy in Brahman."

Mira could not resist, she had to ask "Are you saying
that when I feel tired or frustrated, elated or unhappy, those
feelings are not a part of me? And if so, what are they? Where
do they come from? Why do we have them?"

"That is what Krishna is trying to explain to Arjuna. It is
all a dream, a play. You are no more your frustration than the
clothes you wear are part of your being. Your inner essence is
beyond these"

Mira must have looked sceptical, for he continued:

"You experience this truth every day during your meditations. Have you not noticed that a whole range of emotions come up while you sit. And every single one comes up and then dies down as you sit there unmoved by them. Sometimes you find yourself carried away, in the storm of powerful emotions, thoughts, memories and you think you are these, that they are a part of you. But as your meditation has improved, have you not noticed some other part of you that has been able to stay apart and watch, as if watching a drama unfold on a stage, separate from 'you'. If they were a part of you, without any separate identity, then what is this other part that watches?"

Mira remembered that morning, how while sitting in meditation she had felt irritation when a fly had persistently buzzed around her. But she had told herself that the fly offered an opportunity to practise her focus and watch without getting involved. She had continued to sit calmly as she watched the irritation rise up within herself, a desire to swap the fly or wave it away, an annoyance at its persistence and whining buzz. She had noticed her arm tighten in preparation for reaction. There was a part of her that had wanted to react, another part of her that had watched this part calmly. He was right, there was a part of her that had not been involved in the emotions.

"We call that part the Seer. Meditation is a practise, during which we learn to detach ourselves from the veil, from the outer garments of our soul if you like, layer by layer we approach our real Self. We aim to live each moment of our lives abiding in the Seer, watching as the world unfolds around us and knowing that our emotional responses are not us, we can watch them and stay uninvolved. They are part of the play taking place on this stage, around us. They are not us."

"It's not about controlling emotions or suppressing them. It's about knowing you are not them, they are not you, separating yourselves from them and remaining unaffected"

It was an unusually hot and dry day and Mira felt tired, her energy sapped by the sun. She had not slept well the previous night and for the past few days she had not been able to shake a strong desire to go back home, at least for a while. She could not help wander what was happening there and she was afraid of what she might find when she returned after such a long absence.

She was annoyed and a little surprised that her previous emotions of bliss and wanting to remain here forever and her other world seeming unreal and insignificant had all suddenly flipped over. But she was beginning to realise that is the nature of things. Our emotions, thoughts, sense of wellbeing can flip so suddenly and sometimes without any obvious reason.

She felt like she had reached a point of saturation. Her brain was full, her limbs aching from the long hours of stillness and she missed food, tasty, spicy, different food. She missed coffee. She missed the freedom of being able to do whatever she wanted to, whenever she wanted. And she missed variation, she craved change. Being able to get up and go to bed when she wanted to, choosing what she did when.

On the other hand, a part of her knew that this was all part of a desire to escape. It was hard work staying here and facing her inner world, having no distractions, no outlet. She did not want to surrender and give up. She had reached a point in her practise where she was much more aware and the resistance to continuing was strong. A part of her wanted to escape to an easy life, an unaware, ignorant way of being. Perhaps her ego was already gathering its troops to prevent the peaceful and wise from taking over.

She remembered she had Pixie to help her when she needed and decided to ask for help. That afternoon she found a secluded spot in the gardens and wished for Pixie to appear.

Pixie was with her in a flash, smiling as always.

"What shall I do, Pixie", her voice practically a moan. "I want to go back, but I also want to stay. What will I find when I return? Do I even still have a home there? And am I just trying to escape? Is this yet another failure of mine? Shouldn't I stay and see this through? Can you help me? Can you give me the strength, will power, conviction, whatever it is I need to keep me here and get this done?"

"First the logistical part of your question, Mira. You can return to whatever you wish to find. You can go back to the morning you left if that's what you want. Don't worry about the world you've left behind. And as for giving you what you need to stay, I can't do that. You need to decide for yourself whether it's better for you to stay or leave, and when. But the way you asked your questions strikes me. Too many should's, and ought's and the word failure too. Nothing is a failure. If you need to go back, do so and respect your decision to do so, knowing it's what you need. Not everything is a test of your spirit. There is nothing you should or ought to do. You choose what is best for you at this moment, and then respect your decision. Try to make it knowing why. That way you won't have regrets afterwards."

"But this is getting too much for me. I need a break"

"Why not speak to one of your teachers about this? Do you think that you're the first person who has felt this way? You humans are funny. You all go through similar emotions and yet you all think each experience you go through and each emotion you feel is unique and end up suffering alone. You are all unique, yes, but what you feel, in some different shade perhaps, but in essence the same, is felt by every other one of you. Stop keeping yourself from the others. You're all human aren't you? Open up, share and you'll find you're greeted with more understanding and support than you'd ever imagined. This is a process and many others have been down this road before you. Why not ask for some advice? You can then decide if you want to take the advice, or how much of it you feel applies to you. But first you need to reach out."

"But Pixie, I am different. Is this even a real world? I come from somewhere else, a different time, a different place, a different life…"

"You're missing the point of what I just said. First of all, this world is no less real than the one you left behind and neither are these people. Try it out Mira. Ask them your questions. Tell them how you feel. Speak to them, the teachers, the students. Be totally honest and open. The teachers are there to guide and support you and the students are all here, in it with you, you're in this learning experience together"

"Okay, I'll try". Mira was not convinced and the thought of opening up and speaking about her feelings did not appeal to her. But a glimmer of hope was appearing at the same time. If Pixie was right, they could help her through this. She was determined to try anyway. Was she not here to experience this life fully after all? And what did she have to lose?

We are not alone. We all hold the Divine spark within us and we all cry, laugh, feel loneliness, pain and joy. We all want to be happy, feel loved and appreciated. Why surround ourselves with barriers, when all we need to do is reach out and let go of our self-created isolation.

"Krishna, the mind is restless, turbulent, powerful, violent; trying to control it is like trying to tame the wind." Arjuna to Krishna in the Bhagavad Gita, VI:34, translation by Eknath Easwaran

Krishna replies: "It is true that the mind is restless and difficult to control. But it can be conquered, Arjuna, through regular practise and detachment. Those who lack self-control will find it difficult to progress in meditation; but those who are self-controlled, striving earnestly through the right means, will attain the goal." Bhagavad Gita VI:35-36, translation by Eknath Easwaran

She didn't have to wait for very long for an opportunity. After the next lecture she noticed a teacher standing close by. So she took the opportunity, walked a few steps up to him and spoke before she could change her mind. "May I ask you something?"

"Of course"

"I'm struggling with…" she wasn't sure how to describe what she felt. "I feel unsettled. Sometimes I have an urge to run away. Sometimes all of the sitting, focusing,… well, actually having to be with myself with nothing to do, nothing to shut out the noise in my head, the anxiety I feel in my chest,… sometimes it's all a bit too much, I feel too much. I wonder if I'm not ready, or I'm doing something wrong, or there's something wrong with me. Why is this so difficult for me. Others are tranquil. They're not struggling. They're happy. That happiness touches me sometimes, but mostly I'm not happy, or tranquil. I'm not even focused. I'm not even meditating. I'm just unsettled, irritated and angry. I understand what you said this morning. In my mind I do. And I accept the truth of it. But that's not how I feel. At least, not most of the time. Sometimes I feel like I could explode and all I want to do is run away. And my brain has turned to mush. So much information, I don't know if I can take in any more. What's wrong with me? What am I doing wrong? Should I even be here at all?"

He gazed at her with such a gentle, compassionate expression on his face, she thought her heart would break. He made her want to cry, or something in his expression did. He showed love, not judgement, surprise, impatience nor any other such emotion she had been expecting from him. And in fact, although she forced herself to hold them back, a few tears started to linger under her eyelids and ease their way down her cheeks. She felt so much relief, after all her pent up anxiety, frustration and worry. It was like a lid had been lifted and the densely packed gaseous liquid was about to burst out.

"I feel so alone" she said and with that, there was no restraining the tears anymore. She started to cry freely, her shoulders sloped in, her hands went up to her eyes and she was sobbing loudly. As she sobbed uncontrollably, her mind was still running, ordering her to stop being such a child and pull herself together, wondering what he must think of her, feeling embarrassed and ashamed and angry with herself. A torrent of thoughts that had no effect on her tears at all. Uncomfortable minutes passed by, with her mind fighting her tears and her tears forcing their way through anyway. But gradually her tears eased, they became gentler and she was able to breathe.

He waited patiently until the force of her emotions had died down, then he placed a hand on her shoulder. The pressure was welcome; gentle, warm, and strong. She felt herself steady under his reassuring contact. She looked up and was amazed to see depths of compassion and care in his eyes. Her tears stopped.

He started to speak, slowly, gently. "We've all been there Mira" he said. He knows my name, she thought, amazed and grateful. "Why don't you take a break? You've been doing so well, you can allow yourself a little time off" Her mind recoiled "doing well? What the hell is he talking about? I've just told him how badly I've been doing."

As if reading her mind he added "Believe me you have been doing extremely well. As I said, we have all been there. It's a struggle, pretty much all the way. All those faces that look so serene and happy, it took those people many, many years to reach where they are now. And out of all the hundreds of people that attempt meditation, despite all their best intentions and strong promises, they give up much more easily. What you are doing is difficult for everyone, no exceptions, but with practice, perseverance and patience you can reach serenity too."

"But then why should I take break? Can't you offer me guidance and help so that I can continue?"

"You can continue. But all the guidance has already been given. The rest is up to you. In a way it's simple. All you need to do is continue. And yet it is extremely hard, because there are no magic wands, shortcuts, or painless paths. And every part of you wants to run. You can choose to struggle on, take a break and come back, or give up completely. The choice is yours. No one else can go through the struggle for you. We all have to go down our own path ourselves. And although we are all supported and guided by our teachers, our community and God, only we ourselves can actually fight our own war. We can't do it for anyone else and they can't do it for us."

"And if I did take a break, what should I do during it to make my return easier and definite? I'll be left alone with myself, and with time. I don't know if I can handle me. I'll get distracted by 'life'. I don't even know if I'll have enough conviction or strength to return."

At this he laughed. "Wise words indeed. Most people run away from themselves, their inner lives and don't even know they're doing it. Their entire life becomes a flight from what's within. They ignore their inner feelings that they are unsettled and unfulfilled, with something missing in their lives. They avoid the void by constantly keeping themselves busy, layering their inner being with stresses, plans, hopes, dreams, activity. Anything so that they don't have sit with their feelings, with the growing emptiness inside. They have an infinite number of reasons not to sit and every day they find new ones, not aware that they're perpetually running. At least you know that is what's driving your desire. It's what brought you here in the first place, isn't it? They bury their heads and keep going on. You stopped, lifted your head and asked questions. When we need help, it always comes, sometimes from completely unexpected places. When we ask questions, the answers always come, as long as we are watching out for them and are open enough to see them, even when they are unexpected or undesired replies.

That is why you're here Mira. You have courage and strength. You're open and curious. Believe me, you are doing very well indeed. Just be compassionate with yourself. What you feel, the anger, the wondering what's wrong with me, the irritation, it is all normal. It's all part of the process. See it for what it is. It is your ego rearing its army, ready to defend the illusion of what you have always thought of as who you are with everything it has. We all have that, but some, like you, question it and others never do and live and die in ignorance, unfulfilled, never satisfied, never truly happy and they either never wonder why, or if for a moment they do, they push the thought away quickly. We fear death and the ego fears it most. All kinds of emotions come up, and they become especially obvious when we meditate, because we can't hide them behind work, activities, thinking. We get to know them. They want to take us back into their fold, just so we can't keep peeling them away. They fear death so put up a big show of force.

Just acknowledging that and continuing is victory. Simply continuing to sit is the final victory. They cannot win over that. But you need to be kind with yourself. Acknowledge what you feel and let yourself do what you feel you need to do. Don't force. When you force, you tire yourself, you strengthen them, and that is not good."

Mira thought for a while, but she still was not clear about her path. Was it different? Staying would be forcing. He had told her staying would be victory, but then told her not to force. She couldn't have it both ways. So which one was the 'right' choice for the moment? "But I have no idea what I should do"

"You said should. There are no shoulds. What does your heart need? What does it ask for?"

"It needs to run and scream and not feel"

"Well then, run and scream and try not to feel, although that last one might be harder to attain."

"What do people who want a break do here? Or am I the only one?"

"You are never the only one Mira. We are all the same in a way, as different as we might all appear on the surface. And they do whatever they need to do. Some give up and leave. Some go home and return. Some just wander off for a few days. Maybe all you need is to be away from the group for a day or two. Or simply not take part in the meditation. Go for your run then. Do what you want. Stay aware whatever you do. Notice what happens, inside. If you don't feel settled during and after, check your thoughts. Are they punishing you for your choice? Don't let them. Make your choice as wisely as you can in the moment and once you set out on a course of action, make the most of that action. Enjoy it. If you decide it was not the right course, change it. But never punish yourself for your choice. That is self harm. Look at it, analyse it by all means and decide on the next move. Let the past one go once you have learned what it was there to teach you."

Mira thought for a moment, then added "Most of all, I want to not feel alone"

"You are not alone, you just think you are"

"I feel I am"

"Fine. You feel you are. Doesn't change the fact that you are not. We all have the same essence, the same Divine light within us. And covering that, we all have a colourful collage of a mixture of the same emotions, in different proportions and shades, felt and expressed in different ways, but the same illusions nonetheless. We all want to be happy, we all strive for whatever we think will bring us happiness, even though what we think will make us happy quite often does not. We all try to avoid pain. We reach for what we like and shun what we do not. We fear when we are threatened and anger when we feel fear or when we think we will not get what we want.

You are uncomfortable with what you see come up and you fear letting go, as you have always believed yourself to be a combination and sum of what you think you are and what you feel. So you want to run when you don't like what you see. You have not yet really understood they are not you. You have not yet learned acceptance and letting go. You want to avoid uncomfortable emotions and the discomfort of sitting with them makes you angry. So tell me, how are you different in all this? We all have the same problems when we walk down a spiritual path.

But then, you needn't force. Forcing things down makes them more powerful and wastes your energy and joy. If you need to run, notice that need, notice it gather into energy and strength in your body, the way your muscles tense up, the warmth that spreads in your limbs. If you still need to run, run and watch how you feel during and after.

If you feel alone, speak to others. You will find that you are not at all alone.

There is nothing wrong with what we feel, as long as we don't get carried away by those feelings, harm ourselves by fighting them or punishing ourselves for having them. It is not the emotions that are good or bad, right or wrong, it is us thinking that they are so and that we are those emotions and then acting on them that makes them so. And that includes berating ourselves for having them. They are just harmless forms of energy without any of the qualities we allocate to them inherently a part of them. It's our judgement that tends to pile loads on them. Anger is a condensation of energy that builds up and becomes dense in your muscles. That is all it is. It is what you do with or against that energy that causes suffering to you or others."

"When the senses contact sense objects, a person experiences cold or heat, pleasure or pain. These experiences are fleeting; they come and go. Bear them patiently, Arjuna. Those who are not affected by these changes, who are the same in pleasure and pain, are truly wise and fit for immortality. Assert your strength and realise this!" Krishna speaking to Arjuna in the Bhagavad Gita, II:14-15, translation by Eknath Easwaran

Mira did not go for a run, or take a day off. The drive to do so lost its power with her conversation. The next day she felt calmer and her meditation was the strongest she had experienced so far. She had been listened to and even more importantly, she had been heard. She had received compassion, respect, acknowledgement and love. She did not feel alone in the group any longer and that made a huge a difference to the way she felt inside. She joined conversations during their breakfast and her face was lighter, opening out into a smile more often. She realised how much she had kept herself from the others, feeling so apart from them and so increasing her sense of exclusion. As soon as she joined in their conversations, she found herself welcomed. For the first time she started to feel a part of the community.

Throughout the day, whenever she felt an emotion rise up, she reminded herself she was not that emotion and if she watched, it would simply pass her by.

When, in the future, she looked back on that conversation, she was always amazed at the power having compassion for and simply listening, really listening, to someone in need had.

One morning she had a very direct experience of the concept stated in the Bhagavad Gita II:14-15. She felt a momentary light of wisdom dawn within her. A result of direct experience and understanding of her experience, deep in her body and soul.

She was sitting in meditation as usual and her right knee was aching. She tried to ignore the pain, but it seemed to get louder, demanding her attention. Then her left foot went numb and she had pins and needles all the way up her leg. She was in a lot of discomfort. And out of nowhere the thought entered her mind "everything has a beginning, middle and end. These are just sensations, they will pass. Watch them."

So she did, without moving to ease her discomfort. She watched her foot with interest, dissecting the different sensations. The dull ache, the odd pin prick, the desire to move her foot. Although her foot was numb, there was stuck energy in there somewhere, wanting to burst out into movement. She noticed a throbbing sensation emerge and she thought "and so it's already starting to change". She could feel blood pump into different parts of her body. The discomfort increased. The foot was crying out for movement. She refused to give in to it and continued to watch. A sensation from the sole of her foot started to spread out, like little bursts of energy wanting to jerk her foot into motion. She resisted the impulse and still she watched. The little bursts became weaker and just as they were easing off, her big toe started to twitch from the inside. A wave of energy went up her body, wanting to express itself as a scream. Then another wave. Her arm caught her attention and she started to watch that.

For a moment she took her attention back to her foot, but it had gone quiet. Instead it was now her arm that was distracting her and Mira realised how demanding they all were, constantly trying to distract her away from the connection she was trying to build and maintain with her innermost core, her Divine essence.

Knowing them for what they were, physical sensations, impulses, nothing but distractions, separate from her, sensations that appeared, changed, disappeared, changed, appeared elsewhere, changed, disappeared, and her gradually growing understanding of the philosophy behind human nature, changed her attitude to what she was experiencing,

111

which changed her habitual responses to discomfort, which, in short, changed everything. She no longer felt compelled to react. No longer felt discomfort, just curiosity and amazement at what was unfolding.

All these sensations that she had always assumed were her, a part of her, needs, drives, experiences, they were nothing but clouds, floating by, changing shape moment by moment as she watched.

Her heart became light and she took her focus back to her chosen focus point for that morning's meditation. Her focus deepened and she found a sense of ease and comfort in her body and a focus in her mind that was new to her, a so far not experienced depth and level of simply, beautifully, peacefully just being. Her breath became subtle and gentle and she smiled, with heartfelt joy.

It became easier after that to remind herself whenever a physical, mental or emotional disturbance came up, that they too would pass, no matter how forceful or strong, that they were interesting to watch, but nothing more and nothing personal. Her immediate personal experience had brought her theoretical knowledge to the forefront, much more easily accessible and applicable for her at all times. All sensations, discomforts, thoughts, feelings, of any intensity, variety or level of pleasantness or unpleasantness float by eventually. And even as they were there, they changed and shifted, keeping the experience of watching them fresh and interesting through the duration. They had nothing to do with her, not really, not with her true Self. Her true Self watched as they played on. They tried to hang on, to feed off of her weak mind, to settle in and make a home for themselves, but Mira, at least in that moment and for the duration of that moment, had freed herself from them. These days, more often than not, she could simply let them pass by.

With practise, it became easier. The knowledge that they would pass by if she let them came faster and became more of a habit. The more it happened, the more natural it became.

The habit started to permeate her daily life. When she felt hungry, she thought 'just a sensation' and noticed its quality. When she felt bored, she detached herself and thought 'just another sensation, notice' and more and more of the moments in her life became a play of awareness, of watching and disentangling herself from lifelong patterns, emotions, beliefs and assumptions.

"Even the wise man acts according to the tendencies of his own nature. All living creatures go according to Nature; what can (superficial) suppression avail? Attachment and repulsion of the senses for their specific objects are Nature-ordained. Beware the influence of this duality. Verily these two (psychological qualities) are one's enemies!" Bhagavad Gita III:33-34, translation by Paramahansa Yogananda

Days were getting shorter and greyer and the wind could get pretty menacing at times. They were all feeling the cold. Additional layers of clothing had been handed out, but even these were not enough to keep the chill of approaching winter out of their bones. Mira wondered how they would manage once winter truly set in.

One morning, after an especially painful meditation session, during which every part of her body felt cold and her limbs went numb quickly, when she thought she might freeze in her seat and her brain felt achy and her bones were stiff, she started gazing around. Every muscle in her body was hurting and she could not extract her mind from the pain she was feeling, especially in her hands and feet. She noticed that others were struggling too. The warming smile of the sun visited them ever less frequently. She was feeling especially irritated with herself and the weather that morning. What was the point of it all. How she wanted to be snuggled up under warm covers, in front of a roaring fire, a cup of hot tea between her hands. A warm bath would have been better than heaven itself. And all of this was within her reach. She would not even have to trudge through winter slopes along frosty cliffs to reach them. A passing thought and she could be as warm as she wanted to be. But challenges were always appealing to Mira. Partly because they brought out her strength and will power and partly because somewhere inside she still believed she deserved hardship and punishment and part of her got a ridiculous sense of satisfaction out of struggling and being beaten about by difficulties.

"If I don't freeze to death", she thought, "I will surely catch a horrendous cold". Someone close by moved in their seat, they could not settle either. "How can we focus in meditation when even our basic needs are not met", wondered Mira.

She forced herself to stay still for a little longer, but it was no use. Her mind, that had been fighting her sensations of discomfort, her defeatist attitude and angry thoughts, was now completely fixated on her pain and overwhelmed by the harsh daggers she was plunging into herself. All she wanted to do was leave. Her thoughts were demanding she leave, making excuses, raging at the place, the cold, the insensitivity of the teachers, the annoying participants,… Those thoughts grew louder and louder until she could hear nothing else.

She decided she was better off leaving the meditation space before she exploded. She got up, not as quietly as she had meant to, and walked off. But that made things worse. As soon as she had gained enough distance between herself and the group, her mind started raging at herself even more abusively. She was such a failure. Why could she not be calmer, more at peace? She was obviously not progressing and not at all fit for this place or this company. She felt disappointed with herself, furious and upset. She did not know whether she was about to burst into tears or start screaming abuse at the wind.

"They're obviously not good teachers" she thought, "otherwise they would know how to help me". She realised she was trying to scatter blame around and with renewed gusto her anger and blame returned back onto herself.

"It's no use" she thought, "I have to leave". But the obstinate part of herself refused to admit failure. "Maybe they can help, just wait one more day. Remember it will pass"

Her morning passed in discomfort and she was grateful when she heard the gong sound for breakfast. She returned to the group, still irritated and impatient. There was not much

115

chit chat going on today. Everyone was subdued, wrapped up in their layers of clothing and shawls. No one looked especially happy and there were certainly no audible prayers of gratitude for what they had today. And again she wondered what they were really achieving. If they were gaining deeper peace and contentment, she could not see it now.

She felt someone's elbow against her chest and before she had time to realise what she was doing, her elbow jerked up and pushed the woman. The woman looked startled and then angry and Mira faced her, ready to fight her ground if need be, but the woman turned away.

As she sat down to eat, Mira could not have felt more dejected. She hated herself even more, if such a thing was possible, for her aggressive reaction. She felt a blanket of hatred rise up in her and wrap itself thickly around her heart and soul. It was too powerful, she could not bear to watch it. It assertively and firmly took over. And then suddenly she was crying, out of frustration, anger, discomfort, abject loneliness, cold and fatigue. She was no longer aware of her surroundings, she cried into her bowl, not even aware of how loud her sobs were.

As her tears grew scarcer and the force of her sobs subsided, Mira noticed someone sitting near her, watching her. She looked up. There was such a tender, compassionate look on her face, Mira thought she would burst into tears again. But the source of her tears had been exhausted, at least for the time being.

When her sobs had settled down sufficiently, the woman spoke. She was one of the teachers there, although Mira was not very familiar with her.

"Come. Let's go for a walk".

Mira obeyed. They walked in silence for a while. Mira felt too defeated and tired from her outburst to talk at first, but eventually the thought nearest the surface blurted out.

"I can't do this."

"But you are 'doing' it. You're here, you're breathing, you're doing your best"

"But I'm failing at everything miserably. I felt so angry this morning. I was angry with everyone, especially myself, and that's okay in a way, it harms no one but me. But I was furious with everyone else too, my teachers, and every single person here, regardless. I reacted badly and aggressively towards a woman just before we ate and my anger was so full, I could have easily hit her. I thought meditation brought calm. Instead it seems to make me angrier and more irritable than I ever was"

"First of all, you might have felt like it, but you did not hit the woman you refer to."

"No thanks to me. She turned away, so there was no one there to hit."

"Listen, Mira. You've heard this many times, but I want to reassure you. It's all a part of the process. It's not that you're angrier or more irritable now than you were before. If anything those feelings were always there, buried within you. And if it's any consolation, we all have those thoughts and feelings. As we quieten our minds, gradually deeper layers of our being come to surface and show their face. You're just seeing more of what was previously hidden that's all. They will evaporate over time."

"But in the mean time, I'm going to go mad. It's too much. I don't know how to handle them" Even as she said this, she was realising the truth of what the teacher was telling her. She had always noticed moments of unexplained anger or irritation, coming out of nowhere. Sometimes she would only notice after the moment had passed and she had already reacted inappropriately, regretting it thoroughly afterwards.

"You are handling them. There's no magic trick you can use to make them vanish. You need to face what comes up, watch if you can, and they will pass. Try not to get involved with them. If they're too strong to be with and watch, go for a walk, do some work, something, anything, until their strength has diminished. Berating yourself only feeds the anger, try not to fall into that trap. "

"Easy for you to say. I was beyond even thinking about trying just now and that's not the first time, although it was the strongest I can think of."

"It gets easier"

Exasperation started to rise in her voice. Her initial gratitude for the compassion and warmth the teacher had shown was giving way to annoyance and anger. She did not feel heard or understood. Who was this woman anyway. "That's what everyone keeps saying, but it's not getting easier for me. I'm cold and tired and I've had enough. I thought I was getting better at it. I was more focused, more content, happier. But now that's all gone and instead I've become a ball of irritation and anger."

The woman was silent for a while, perhaps she was pausing, feeling Mira's rising resentment, then said gently "we all say that, because we've all been there. You wouldn't be alive if you had no more emotions. They are part of our outer sheaths, part of being human. We all feel anger, frustration, joy. We all like some things and don't like others. We all feel tired and irritated, we…"

Mira cut her short rudely "yes, but every class we're being told how to face everything with equanimity, how to watch without getting carried away, how to let go of likes and dislikes and not get controlled by them. Well, it's not working for me. I've been here long enough to be able to say that I have tried and I have failed." She practically added, "So there!"

The teacher was tempted to let it go. Mira was not willing to listen or hear, at least not right now, but she decided to give it one last try nonetheless. Something in Mira's angry desperation asked to be reached out to, to be touched, heard, felt. "There's no such thing as failing in this. It's a process. Some days are better than others, easier, more peaceful. Some days we struggle more than we think we could bear until it is finally over and we look back on our turmoil. It's an uphill journey. It does get better and easier over time. But no one says it will be easy all the time, or even most of the time.

You're becoming more aware of all that lies within you. Is it not worth it even just for that? First those layers need to be exposed. We peel off the outer layers away one at a time. Then the ones beneath those and then the ones beneath those ones. Until we reach our core. Unfortunately we can't just rip them all off in one go. There are lifetimes of layers covering your Self, there to protect and shield you. They have most probably saved you many times in the past. But then they make a home in your being and become habits you fall into even when they are no longer helpful, even when they harm. It takes time and effort and diligence to remove these layers, small bit by small bit. And most of all, it takes patience. Have faith in the process and that God will help and guide you always. Have compassion towards yourself."

"I feel like giving up"

"And what happens then? You can't unlearn what you have learned and erase what you have experienced"

"I could go home" Mira mumbled quietly.

Silence followed. Then the woman said "yes, you can"

The obvious statement sapped all of Mira's remaining energy out of her. "Why?" she said, but did not expect an answer.

She did not join any of the classes that day. She needed to be away from the group. She was afraid of reacting badly again, but even more than that, she was afraid of the power of her emotions and desperately needed a break from them. She did not want to face them, and so she distracted herself.

She wished for Pixie once again and Pixie duly appeared.

"What shall I do Pixie?"

"Ride it out Mira. If you leave now, you'll regret it and struggle to forgive yourself. Trust your teachers. Have more faith in yourself. Have more love. Love is our true nature, not anger. Anger will pass, love is always there, it is part of your essence. But you need to allow yourself to access it. You need to learn to love yourself first. Only when you learn to love and forgive yourself can you let love for all blossom."

"It's hard to love someone with so much shit in them" Mira remarked. "I wouldn't love me if I met me right now."

"You think others feel that way about you? You believe they don't love you? You think they see you as you see yourself? You would be so surprised little one if you could live in someone else's thoughts for a day, or even just an hour. Everyone sees themselves in a way that's different from how others perceive them. You need to learn to forgive, especially yourself. No person is perfect, so why place the demand of perfection on yourself? Is that fair? Would you see someone else struggling with meditation as a failure, or would you feel compassion and understanding towards them? Who do you think you are anyway that you should be perfect when no one else is? You don't expect perfection from anyone else and you love them warts and all. Why can't you give that to yourself as well? Forgiveness first, the rest will follow. There is nothing wrong with you, nothing bad about you. Your reactions are a play of different energies, mixed in and grown over many lifetimes. They're veils covering your soul. It takes time to let them go. Time, patience, compassion, love and diligence. They are not your essence. They will change. They are not important. Let the events of this morning go. Don't cling on to your resentment. Remember, when you dwell on something, you feed it. Don't feed your anger. Do you hate yourself for feeling pain in your foot?"

"Of course not, but that's not within my control, and it doesn't harm anybody"

"Your emotions are no more within your control than the weather. What you do with your emotions is what you have choice over. If you choose to be angry with yourself for getting irritated, then you add to your negative feelings and feed them. You can equally choose to forgive yourself, knowing it's a part of human nature to feel these things. Let it go. You are not bad for feeling anger any more than you are for having white skin or an aching shoulder. How can you let these emotions pass if you cling on to them so strongly by punishing and hating yourself?

"So just accept? That's what you're saying. Accept and forgive"

"Yes, even yourself, especially yourself. Do you not believe God loves you and every single other being in the universe exactly as we are? Do you think He judges or dislikes? No! So allow yourself to receive and accept some of that love and compassion."

Mira felt calmer. She understood and believed Pixie's words, but could not feel their truth in her body. She knew she would be able to as soon as she had had some rest and a little distance between herself and the morning's events had come to pass. Maybe the rest would also come.

"Learn to forgive yourself, so you can forgive others. Learn to love yourself so you can love others. Be as kind to yourself as you would like to be and mostly are to others"

"There's no turning back now, is there Pixie? Now that I've experienced this place and learned what I have, I will never be able to go back to not knowing"

"That's true. You might not feel it now, but you will appreciate it some day"

"It's going to be a rough ride"

"You might think that things were better before, but they weren't. You were just less aware of what was missing. You were searching for something Mira. At some level everyone is. You have found your path, but now you're daunted by it. Don't be. You're supported through this process and always will be. Have faith"

Mira knew in her heart she had no choice. This was the route she had chosen, consciously or not and she knew she was meant to be there. She joined the group for the last few hours of the day, all her emotions drained out, her mind numb and empty, her body ready to drop from fatigue.

"The cognisor of truth, united to God, automatically perceives, "I myself do nothing" – even though he sees, hears, touches, smells, eats, moves, sleeps, breathes, speaks, rejects, holds, opens or closes his eyes – realising that it is the senses (activated by Nature) that work amid sense objects. Like unto the lotus leaf that remains unsullied by water, the yogi who performs actions, forswearing attachment and surrendering his actions to the Infinite, remains unbound by entanglement in the senses." Bhagavad Gita V: 8-10, translation by Paramahansa Yogananda

Much to her surprise, she woke up feeling lighter the next morning. The turmoil of the previous day had evaporated with the night. She felt immense relief. She felt so settled and at peace with everything that at that moment she could have sworn that she could stay there forever, happily ever after. She chuckled at the transience of it all. "Everything does pass" she thought and prepared herself for the morning meditation with enthusiasm, knowing that this sense of joy and elation too would pass.

They were not led to the side of the ocean that morning. Instead they all gathered around a burning fire, surrounded by trees. The trees created a protective wall around them, breaking off the intensity of the cold wind and providing a welcome sanctuary. "Even better" Mira thought, "positive attitude and things on the outside are already changing for the better". She settled down for meditation finding a spot near a vast old tree. She felt safe and held by it, as if it had reached mighty big, warm, soft arms out and took her into its caress.

Her meditation was deeper than usual and she felt at peace. She could feel the tree's calming energy soothe her. The connection she felt to the tree, and through it to nature and through nature to her soul and through her soul to the universe and Divine was strong and beautiful. She felt nourished and satisfied. Her focus was better than usual and she was pleased with this turn of events. In fact everything was going better that morning. She enjoyed her breakfast, taking time as she chewed each mouthful, taking pleasure in the texture and taste of the usual brown sludge. She was awake, alert, aware and focused during classes and seemed to understand more of what was being said, not only the words in her mind, but their meaning in her soul. By lunch time she felt satisfied that she was making progress at last.

She had been initiated into Kriya Yoga only a few days ago and she found it easier to practise than simply watching her breath and sensations, thoughts and feelings that came up. There was a movement, something concrete to focus her mind on, more detail to be attentive to and the movement of energy up and down her spine felt accessible to her, something to bring her focus back to when her mind wondered, something watchable, tangible. She was able to keep her focus on her meditation object with more ease. It proved to be a method that absorbed her mind more fully.

Her evening ritual of thinking back over her day and analysing how she had done on her internal battlefield had started to make more sense to her too. Gratitude flowed through her when things went well and gradually day by day she was finding more and more to be grateful about. "Things aren't so bad after all" she thought to herself.

She stayed close to the ever-lit fire and the group all day, not feeling the need to withdraw and isolate herself. Her usual drive for a change of space and need for solitude were not there. She found herself in conversation with an older man in the evening. She had barely noticed him before. Whenever she had seen him, he had given her the impression of being in a meditative state, whether eating or strolling around the grounds he gave out a sense of calm and inner focus at all times. He seemed to blend in with his surroundings and stayed unnoticed most of the time. But now that she had noticed him, she was curious about him and his life.

"How long have you been here?" she asked when their conversation paused, which up to that point had flowed easily as they discussed the material they had learned in class that day. She found he had an amazingly deep understanding of what had been said and upon further enquiry Mira realised that he had read and studied this subject many times. When she asked him if he never grew tired or bored of it, he was completely surprised. "How could anyone get bored of such a vast and deep subject? Every single time I read one of those verses I understand, feel and learn something new. It grows in depth and reveals more". That felt important to Mira. She feared boredom quite possibly more than anything else in the world. She got bored too easily and lost interest in a flash. She didn't want that to happen with her new found passion. Nothing she could think of would ever replace what she felt and learned here and the sense of growing and maturing she received from it. If she lost this passion, which filled her life more than anything else ever had done and gave her more satisfaction and her life more meaning than anything else she had experienced, she was not sure what else she would do. There would be no meaning left in her life and nowhere else to look where she might find some.

"Many many years" he replied, seemingly oblivious to passing time. She felt quite sure that he would not have been able to answer the question accurately.

"Did you ever struggle? Did you want to leave?"

"Of course I did. And yes, not only did I want to leave, but I did leave."

"What happened?"

"It got too much. I hated myself, I hated this place, I thought I was going mad. I probably was going mad in a way. I couldn't stand it any longer. But although I might have left this physical place, I found I took myself with me: the hatred, the difficulties, what I had learned and felt and what was still missing. So all I did was move myself to a different location, one which did not have any of the support and guidance offered here, and continued with the worst part of my experiences: the confusion, pain, anger… I don't think any one of us can leave ourselves behind and move on, not once we've travelled some distance and have become aware enough to not be able to ignore the cries… I realised that the source of my discomfort went with me and always would wherever I went. I was either going to kill myself or find a way of dealing with it, facing it. Unfortunately, even though I would have liked to have just ended it, I knew it would not be the end, I would only end up returning to learn the same lessons again and face the same challenges again, bringing my problem self back with me. And maybe next time I would not be so lucky. I might not be offered the opportunity to learn and grow in a place like this, where I'm supported, helped and loved. I figured better to brace myself up, accept whatever help I can get and trudge on as best I can. I had to understand it and work with it rather than trying to run from it. I could never outrun it anyway."

This made sense to Mira. She could return to her old world, but everything that upset her would return with her. The door had been unlocked and opened, she had taken a few steps through and now there was no way of turning back and returning through the now less visible doorway, to the other side and lock it back up.

It then occurred to her that if he could do it, so could she. After all, he had considered taking his life. She hadn't reached that point yet. "I can do it" she thought.

"What helps you most when you struggle?" she asked. Advice from teachers was all very well, but sometimes their advice was beyond her current scope of understanding. She didn't always feel it related to her. They were more advanced and they spoke from their vantage point, not hers. She was hoping for some immediate practical suggestions. "So, for example, if your mind won't quieten down in meditation no matter what you do and how hard you try. None of the methods you know have worked and all kinds of harmful thoughts and feelings start to rage or even worse, you become sure you've failed and it's all pointless and there's something wrong with you and you're too damaged to deserve to go on."

Here Mira had to stop and take a few deep breaths. All that had blurted out of her mouth before she had even realised it was there. But she did find the strength to continue: "What do you do at that moment, to be able to stay seated, to calm yourself down and go back to your focus and not rage in your heart and head?"

"I pray"

Mira was taken aback by the simplicity and directness of his answer. "How do you pray? What do you say? What if I don't believe?"

"Just pray. Faith follows. Pray, help comes. Even the act of uttering a prayer draws you towards your heart. Feel your heart and pray. Pray for guidance, help, support, strength, patience, whatever you want. However you want. Just pray. Or think of things you're grateful for and pray your gratitude. Or think of someone you care about and pray for them if praying for yourself is not easy for you. Or just pray to believe, pray for connection. Doesn't matter for what. Just pray."

They sat in silence again for a few minutes, then he turned to her "None of us, not one of us gathered here now, or any person who has ever lived can do this without help. If you berate yourself for not doing as well as you think you should, that is your ego puffing up its feathers. Thinking that you could do it all on your own is your ego in the first place. You can't! Be humble and ask for help. Look at what part of you demands you be perfect and accomplished. What makes you think you are or ever could be? Give up your ego and your assumption that you should do well. Accept you're a human with thunders and storms raging in your mind and give it all up to God. Offer your meditation to God and offer also your faults. Ask for God's help. What makes you think you can carry all the burden and slay all your mental enemies all by your little self. Let God help. Let God take over. You will feel so much lighter, you'll see. Assuming you should have strength and wisdom enough to take it all on yourself is misguided. Assuming you could be full of love, compassion and patience every moment of the day is delusional. Let God help you"

And then as if as an afterthought he added "Look around you. How can you not have faith. Look at the ocean and the trees, the birds, the sand. Look at the way this whole world is functioning. We humans are the greatest miracle of all. Every cell in our bodies is pulsating, taking in nutrients, using them to serve the body, mutating into organs, bones, tissues as necessary all the time, twenty-four seven. Our minds are more complicated and advanced than any machine that could ever be built. How can you not have faith?"

Mira looked around her, his words striking something inside. How could she doubt. He was right.

"Each prayer is a connection to the Divine, of what is beyond all that we see and sense. Whether you're begging for help, or giving your thanks, no matter what your prayer is, no matter how small or big, it is your bridge to God. Add to it, strengthen it, make it your second nature. Know that God is in everything, including you, and make it your practise to connect to that essence that exists in everything and everyone in the universe. Know that God will hear you no matter what language or method you choose. Know that God is there, always, waiting for us to connect, hoping we will call Him, reach out to Him. Just pray."

Soon after her conversation with the old man Mira sat down, determined to follow his advice. At first she couldn't think of anything to pray for, or what to say, but then it gradually came. Starting with doubt and hesitation, and then ending in full flow with full heart. She offered up her gratitude and prayed for support, help, strength. And as she prayed, her focus moved naturally towards her heart. She continued to sit after her prayers had finished, focusing on her heart centre, feeling it pulsate, feeling its warmth, its energy spreading, opening, at peace.

"It is better to strive in one's own dharma (duty) than to succeed in the dharma of another. Nothing is ever lost in following one's own dharma, but competition in another's dharma breeds fear and insecurity." Bhagavad Gita III:35, translation by Eknath Easwaran

"It is better to perform one's own duties imperfectly than to master the duties of another. By fulfilling the obligations he is born with, a person never comes to grief. No one should abandon duties because he sees defects in them. Every action, every activity, is surrounded by defects as a fire is surrounded by smoke." Bhagavad Gita XVIII: 47-48, translation by Eknath Easwaran

It was a clear, blue morning. Mira saw Pixie as she approached the ocean. She had not wished for her for a very long time. Things had changed, gradually, imperceptibly. She only realised how much when she looked back and compared where she was now to where she had been a few months before. She had changed. She had fully embraced the routine and way of life at the ashram. Meditations seemed to go by quickly and her spare times were spent in meditative contemplation, usually with her face turned to the ocean, enjoying the joyous murmur of the sea and the fresh caress of the wind. She was at ease with herself. Some days were better than others, but overall there was ease and contentment in her being. She had not felt the need to run away for a long time and she had no inclination to go anywhere else or be anyone else.

Pixie's words jerked her out of her comfort though. Said, as always, with a warm smile: "It's time honey"

"Time for what?" her reply came out harsher than she had meant it to. She knew and dreaded the reply.

"Time to go back"

"But I don't want to"

Pixie sat down, gazing out into the distance. Eventually she spoke. "Remember sweet love, you asked me to warn you, prompt or advice you when I deemed it necessary. Well, it is now. We all have our roles to play in life. We have paths set out for us, ones that have been drawn to lead us further and deeper along our individual spiritual paths, towards our essence, towards God. The paths are there for us to learn and grow in wisdom and understanding and bring us closer to our true selves. And each one of us has a different path."

Why was she including herself in this description, Mira wondered. So far she had always talked about human feelings and actions as separate from herself. She did not belong to this world, did she?

But she had more immediate concerns and the question passed on, unasked.

"But is this not my path? It feels like it is. It feels right. This is where I want to be. Did you not say I could wish for whatever I want? You said I could stay or leave as I pleased. This is where I want to be. This is who I want to be. I am at peace. And I am learning.

"I did say you will decide. And you can. It is your choice. But you asked me to guide you and I have come to let you know that there is more for you to do, see and understand. You can stay here if you like, but your path lies elsewhere, and eventually the drive to move towards it will take over anyway. You know there's more. The unease you feel at times asks the same questions, wondering what is next"

"But maybe that's a distraction. I've learned to deal with it just fine. I'm learning and growing. I have found peace. I do not wish to be anywhere else."

"No, but the best path for our spiritual growth is rarely the easiest or most attractive one. It's time for you to take what you have learned back to your old world. Not only to challenge yourself and what you have learned, for it is always harder to be content and at peace always when the world throws so many things at you as the one you come from does. Here it is easier. It is quiet. You are surrounded by spiritual people, all with the same aims, aspirations and hopes. You have no menial, day-to-day concerns, there's no politics or wars, no hunger or humiliation, no suffering before your eyes.

In the stress and confusion of life you will find it harder to live by the precepts you have learned here, but it will teach you even more. Ability to live like this under all circumstances is what you should strive for."

"But if it's harder, I should stay. I'm not experienced or strong enough yet. Why make things harder for myself?"

"You will find a different kind of peace when you feel like you are doing your duty. Your next step is to learn to share, to think of other's wellbeing before yours, to be of service. You have been fortunate and have been given much. Don't you think it's time to give some back?"

Mira was silent. Similar thoughts had occurred to her too, but she had pushed them aside. She didn't want to leave, or make things harder for herself. She didn't trust herself to stay strong through life's challenges or even to be able to keep up her daily meditation. She was realistic. Even if she did continue for a while, life's challenges, hardships and banal existence would eventually take over. She feared her return, her old world would seemed so alien to her now. But she had to accept what Pixie was saying. She was fulfilling her promise, offering guidance even though it was unwelcome.

"I'll leave you for now" Pixie said as she made a move. "Think about what I've said and search your heart. Your heart cannot lie. It will always guide you well. You just need to learn to always listen to it, pay attention and hear. I will not return again unless you ask me to" and with that she was gone, leaving an eerie emptiness where she had been. A vacuum that had suddenly enveloped Mira inside and out and that made her shiver, all the way down into her bones.

Her conversation with Pixie weighed on her mind heavily. Her mood changed. She no longer felt settled where she was. She could not ignore Pixie's advice and her heart's acquiescence. She had asked for guidance after all and she could not complain now that she had received it at a time she would have preferred not to. It would be stupid to ignore it just because she didn't like what she heard. But would she be able to hold true to what she had learned once back there? She wanted to stay, but the seed of her departure had already been sown in her and she could not ignore it.

She decided to speak to one of the teachers. She walked up to one after class. He saw her linger.

"What is it?" he asked gently.

"I need your advice" she said.

They sat down and he watched her face as she struggled to find the right words.

"I feel I need to go back. I mean, I feel I ought to. I don't know how I will, but I need to share what I have learned somehow. I've been told that is my path."

"We all have our duties" he said. We need purpose to our lives. It is good to work for the benefit of others. It'll bring meaning and purpose to your life"

"But I know so little. Here I can learn and practise. Out there…" her words trailed off into the empty air. I'll be lost, she thought.

"You'll be fine. It's a challenge, a far greater challenge to practise out there than it is here. But no one can take what you have learned away from you. Keep it alive within you, close to your heart and be guided by what you have learned in every circumstance. Remember, the Bhagavad Gita was given to us not so that we could all become lofty hermits, but so that we could live amongst others, spiritual or not, in the every day world, working, living, striving, and at the same time staying true to our essence and our practise, helping ourselves and others with its teachings. It's a practical manual above all. It speaks to every aspect of life. It tells us how to live in a moral, spiritual way no matter where we are, what surroundings we find ourselves in, amongst what kind of people, and in everything that we do, no matter what it is. It makes sense for you to take its practise out into the world."

"But am I strong enough? And what do I know anyway? Isn't it better for me to stay here and perfect my knowledge first?"

"For some that is the right way. But for you, obviously not. Something in you calls to take it out there and live back in the world you came from. You cannot ignore that call. Remember what Krishna says, He is within us all, always. Keep your mind on Him through everything you do. Dedicate your return to Him. And teach His words as best you can from your heart. Don't look for completion or perfection. That is God's realm. Do your best, with the most honest and best intentions. That is everything. No more is asked of you."

Mira sighed.

"And pray when you struggle, when you feel lost, when you're making decisions. Pray that you be guided in the right direction, beyond your ego, to do what's right."

Hearing the teacher's clear agreement with what Pixie had said, a heaviness dropped into the pit of her stomach together with acceptance of what she would need to do next and a feeling of resignation. She had hoped he would disagree and tell her it would be best if she stayed. But perhaps this really was the path she needed to set out on now she realised.

"No one's interested in these teachings back where I come from" she said.

"You'll have to find a way to make them interesting and applicable to those you aim to teach. In truth, they are applicable to everyone and you know that. All you need to do is help them see that. Keep it simple. You're in the best position possible to do that, having come from there and lived that life and now having also experienced this. You know and understand them and can make it relatable to them through your own experience."

"Except I never did feel a part of that life, not really. And I never did feel that I understood them." But she knew he was right. "I will do my best" she said eventually.

She stayed on for a few more days, saying final goodbyes to her soul home and the people she had met and grown to love there. After a few days she knew there was no point staying any longer. She was delaying the inevitable. She was only half there anyway, part of her, the resigned part, had already left. So she wished for Pixie with a very heavy heart……

"Avoid a negative approach to life. Why gaze down the sewers when there is loveliness all around us? One may find some fault in even the greatest masterpieces of art, music and literature. But isn't it better to enjoy their charm and glory? Life has a bright side and a dark side, for the world of relativity is composed of light and shadows. If you permit your thoughts to dwell on evil, you yourself will become ugly. Look only for the good in everything, that you absorb the quality of beauty." Paramahansa Yogananda, Sayings of Paramahansa Yogananda

Pixie duly appeared with her usual smile. "You are going to find a deeper sense of contentment in teaching than you could have ever imagined" she said. "It is what you were always meant to do."

Mira nodded, with absolutely no enthusiasm whatsoever , and closed her eyes.

She found herself back in her old room. It felt so cramped and airless now compared to the open ocean air and forest scents. She opened the windows, but instead of the voice of the ocean, she was greeted with traffic noise and fumes, and music coming from one of the other flats, the noise of people rushing around, talking, tyre screeches. Her head filled with noise and felt like it would split in half, breaking apart along ragged lines, causing as much pain as possible while it did. She already missed the quiet and fresh air. She walked back to her bed slowly and slumped on it, too listless to even think.

The next few days she spent in a half dream state. She did not want to be there and at times she didn't feel like she really was. She couldn't find spirit or any enthusiasm within herself to do anything. Getting up was a struggle. She wished for Pixie. This was all her fault after all!

"I don't want to be here" she said.

"You haven't even tried. Give it a chance. Aren't you meant to face life with faith and optimism? Didn't you learn that it is not your outer circumstances that matter but what is inside and how you respond? How does that tie in with your attitude now? You are the same person here as you were there and where you are should not matter. It is especially in these circumstances that your faith and your practise are tested and strengthened." She swept her arm gesturing the room and beyond "none of this really matters".

"It's easy for you to stay. You are not a part of it"

"And you are?"

Mira hated it when Pixie stated the obvious, and yet impossible to grasp.

"So what do I do? Where do I even start?"

"You can start by staying out of bed for more than an hour" Pixie replied. "Go out there. Get to know this world as you did the other ones, as if you had never ever been here before and you are on a temporary trip to learn, experience and live. Wander around, watch, listen. Notice what strikes you. Be open and let go of prior knowledge and judgements, otherwise all you'll see is what you have always seen, but from the worst vantage point because you are approaching it in such a negative attitude. Now come on. I've brought you here using magic so you can see and learn. It's new, because you're new. See it with your meditation eyes, with the same eyes that looked out on to the ocean with so much love. Come on Mira."

Mira nearly countered with "but I already know it in all its forms", but she knew she did not really. She had lived in and experienced this world through her previous mind set and attitudes. Our world is what we see, hear and feel. It is not a separate, objective reality. It is coloured by our feelings, attitudes and viewpoints. It is coloured by our past experiences and our beliefs. And her view point had changed. Surely she had grown and was far more at peace. Anyway, she knew

Pixie was right. If this was going to be her world she would need to look at it through new eyes; fresh, objective eyes. She remembered Pixie's first advice before they had even started on their journeys, "be open". She hadn't even been outside yet and yet she had already painted the whole world outside of her room with colours of judgement, labelled as hard, noisy, bad, hopeless, evil, too far from nature, polluted,… And so the list went on.

She took a deep breath. "Here we go then" she said and started to prepare herself to go out. "Can you stay close?"

"I always am" was Pixie's reply.

She wandered round the streets for a while. It was hard at first. She could not shake her prior knowledge and her feelings of desperate disappointment in this turn of events and the unhappiness she felt. But gradually she was able to look and see, and gradually she was able to become more interested. And suddenly she found she had started to smile."Even this world is beautiful after all", she thought to herself. The snippets of conversation she heard made her smile. She saw a small child playing, naive and happy and Mira's heart warmed. "I can't believe it was that easy. A shift in perception and interested openness was all I needed". But then Mira remembered that that shift had not at all come about easily. In fact if Pixie had not prompted her, she would have never even seen into this. A realisation of the vastness of her chance and how lucky she was to have been offered it with all the support she continued to receive struck her and she prayed in gratitude. That helped her mood even more and she felt as if she was back at the ashram, her heart was full and she was excited, taking in her surroundings, while curiosity and love filled her heart.

She walked into a cafe and looked around herself. She took out a notebook and pen and started to write, starting with her first journey, describing events as they popped up in her memory. And as she wrote, her mind speeding, her hands not able to keep up, the words flowed, taking on a life of their own. She was surprised at how easily the words came to her and how good she felt as she scribbled down everything as fast as she could. A deep sense of peace spread through her. "This is it", she thought." This is how I start."

For the next few weeks she spent most of her time writing. The project had invigorated her. She was happy and woke up each morning excited by the thought of continuing her story. What she wrote took over her mind, her whole being. Even when there was no pen in her hand, in her mind she was still writing. Her writing consumed her and gave her contentment and joy in return for her efforts.

She started to understand what her teacher and Pixie had meant when they talked about purpose in life. It did give her fresh energy and a sense of satisfaction in a way she was not sure she had felt before. She kept at it until her whole story was down on paper. When she was finished, she went out for a walk. Her excitement was still fresh, but she was not sure how to continue next. "What now", she thought. She knew she could keep on writing. The more she wrote, the more ideas came to her. But she also knew that at this point that would only be another form of escapism. She needed to do something with what she'd already created first. She looked around her as if she'd find the answer in her surroundings.

"What now?" she repeated, but this time to Pixie, into thin air. "Can I wish that it be published and read?"

But she knew that would not be right. She knew she would need to put in effort and find a way to do it herself. There are no shortcuts in life and it is good that it is so. We value what we work for. We rarely know the value of what lands in our laps without effort. And also, it is all part of learning. And ultimately that is what life is, that's why we're born and live. To learn. A never-ending process and journey. We are given challenges, struggles, setbacks and pain so that we can grow.

She remembered her teacher say, "when we can truly, in our hearts, be grateful for everything that happens to us, no matter what, how bad it might seem, truly grateful, that's when we reach enlightenment". She could feel the truth of this. Often her mind would tell her to be grateful for everything, and yet her heart did not wish to experience pain or loss, even when her mind told her it was for her benefit, for her growth. She did not want to face hardships. She was not indifferent to pain. Even though her mind knew everything happened for a reason, part of her rebelled against anything she did not want or like.

"Do your duty in the world with optimism, faith and joy" she thought, "whether cleaning the street or ruling the world. Be of service to others"

She leaned back, allowing her back to be supported by the chair, letting her shoulders relax. "The path will appear" she thought.

A woman walked up to her table and motioned to the chair opposite "May I?" she asked. "All tables are taken"

"Of course". She smiled.

The woman placed her cup down and settled into her seat. She looked tired, lines of sternness and fatigue etched into her face. She must have been in her forties. She was thoughtful and sat in silence for a while gazing out into the room, but without really taking in any of her surroundings.

Mira wanted to speak to her, but had no idea what to say, so she started with "it's crowded today for some reason".

"It's always like this on a Saturday" the woman remarked, resentment seeping out through her voice. "Good coffee though"

Mira nodded.

She sat in uneasy silence, wanting to continue talking to the woman, but evidently the woman wanted to keep to herself, so Mira let it go. She got up, smiled to the woman, who did not return her glance or smile and walked out.

She sat in her room looking out of the window, wondering what she should be doing with herself. She went into meditation, struggling to calm her mind at first, but gradually her meditation took over and she was able to sit in peace.

Once she was finished, she felt calm. Her heart knew the next step would come, when the time was right. She was glad she had been able to meditate as she could at the ashram. "Its power is stronger than the effect surroundings have on me" she thought. "It's always available to me and I can always find peace and connection through it. Remember this, Mira, next time you slump into negativity or dullness."

The sun had set and she was sitting in darkness, the noise of traffic was coming in through the open window, but it no longer upset her, it merely brushed past her. Life moved on outside her walls. In a city like this, it never stops. She felt a part of the city, yet separate from it at the same time.

She cleaned her little flat and created, with care, a corner for her meditation, research, reading and practise. She was determined to keep up the practise. It was the most powerful tool she knew of and she was grateful she had been taught it. Her sanctuary ready, she sat in it once more. "This is my mini ashram", she realised. "This corner right now, and it is creatable easily with a rock and a flower if that's all that's accessible to me wherever else I want to have access to it."

When she felt ready, she wished for Pixie's presence and when Pixie appeared she asked "so what now, Pixie? Here I am as you advised, but I'm not clear what I should do next"

"You're being impatient. It will come. One step at a time. Live moment by moment. You're getting lost in what should be, what you should do, what next, the future. Centre yourself in the moment. Meditate. And you'll know what to do next. Try and let go of what next's, should's, ought's…"

"Easier said than done", Mira thought, but she didn't argue. She knew that was the best way to live, but harder to put into action than to talk about. "Not much guidance" she muttered. Pixie smiled. Mira knew it was the best reminder for her at that moment in spite of herself.

Deep down inside we are all the same; we all want to be happy, we all desire love and acceptance and acknowledgement. We all struggle with anger, doubt, fear. Have compassion for all, for we all carry the Divine Spark within our hearts.

"Instead of condemning people, try to understand them. Try to figure out why they do what they do. It breeds sympathy, tolerance and kindness. To know all is to forgive all." Dale Carnegie

Mira became increasingly disciplined with her meditation practise and it became her absolute top priority. This was her time to re-connect with her centre. A time devoted to herself alone, connected to her inner self. Her time for peace, for connection with what was 'real' and essential, the calm, serene place within herself. Each day, no matter how she was feeling, she sat on her meditation cushion and focused. It gave her a sense of structure and belonging, as well as clarity. She felt good about herself for keeping up the discipline. But even more importantly, her meditation became a time dedicated to herself, for herself. She enjoyed it and looked forward to it. She found peace in her practice and a sense of connection not only with God, but also the community she had left behind. Sometimes she even felt a strong sense of connection with the universe. Every morning and evening she sat for an hour and sometimes during the day she sat as well, for shorter periods of time, but they were long enough to re-establish her connection to a sense of calm and clarity.

The next few days she spent looking up publishers. She had to start somewhere. She wrote to a few, sending them a summary of her book, with an introduction message and then she waited. Only one of them replied and she agreed to meet him.

He was an assertive character and she felt uneasy in his presence at first. He shook her hand a little too strongly and his suggestion that she sit sounded more like a command than an invitation. He looked at her with a quizzical expression, as if he didn't believe her, even though she had not yet said anything that could be questioned. He talked over her voice and she found it hard to be at ease in his presence. He was polite and thorough though and did compliment her on her work.

"I enjoyed reading parts of your book" he said. "It's well written. Your language is easy to follow and warm. Your descriptions are vivid. However, the subject matter of your book is, well, quite frankly boring. All this spiritual stuff. Where did it all come from? Do you belong to some kind of society?" This last question was said with special emphasis and a note of condescension in his voice. "People are not interested in reading about this stuff. As well as it is written, your book won't sell" She could hear satisfaction in his voice. He was the one that held power in this relationship and he was enjoying making that very clear to her. He had taken the upper ground by looking down on her work and bringing down her character and believability with one small swoop.

"There must be some people out there who would be interested" Mira replied, without much hope in her voice. She could tell he had already passed judgement and could think of nothing to say that might be worth the energy she would use to utter the words.

"Some, yes, maybe, if your book reaches them that is. It's a tough market." A pause. That statement was meant to convey authority and finality, thought Mira. But for her it was simply uncomfortable.

He followed on with "But I need to make money and this book won't do. You have potential though. Why don't you write something more interesting? Historical thrillers have made a comeback and such a novel would be snapped up, in the hands of a good publishing house that is" meaning his company, his marketing, his publication, and most importantly his idea, his way.

Mira could not help but feel that he got special satisfaction out of belittling her. To him though, he was taking her under his wings, with compassion, offering guidance and help. His ego was pumped up and his chest expanded. Mira half expected him to move his arms up and down like a peacock preparing to surprise with its multicoloured feathers. First she wanted to laugh, but then suddenly she felt repulsed and disgusted by him. She turned her eyes away, not wanting to give away her feelings and not able to bare to look into his arrogant, deceitful eyes for any longer. Mira felt a moment's anger rise in her. She swallowed, closed her eyes and prayed "Dear God, help me feel compassion for him, take away this hatred" Then to herself "It doesn't matter Mira, he doesn't matter, let it go"

She opened her eyes and wondered if there was any point arguing with him, if there was anything at all that she could say which would help her cause or make him question his stance. Why had he even wanted to meet her? He obviously had no interest in what she had written. It was not a thriller, historical or otherwise and Mira knew there was little likelihood she would ever write one. That was not what bubbled up and spoke within her and it was not what she felt driven to share.

"Give it a go" he added. "Maybe read a few to help inspire you."

Mira was quiet. A copy of her book sat quietly between them, a heavy weight pulling her down. Once more she wondered to herself, what next and had to shake herself out of the dull, empty feeling that was gradually taking over. In spite of the dislike she felt towards this man, although she had no respect for him or his opinions at all, the heavy fog was descending.

"Don't take it so badly" he added. "Most people struggle for years to get their work published and even then success is rare. Those stories you hear of overnight fame and wealth, they never really happen, not that way. Usually it takes years, sometimes decades of effort, heartbreak and perseverance."

"Fame and wealth are not what I'm after", she thought, but there would be no point saying that to him. For him they were the essence of life, the only things worth striving for, nothing else would make sense in his mind.

"Thank you for your advice" she said. "And your compliment"

"That's a girl" he chuckled. "Tell you what, why don't you come over for dinner this Saturday?"

Again Mira wondered why. He didn't like her book and was not going to publish it, so why take this time to meet her and why invite her over? He didn't think that highly of her after all. But he had liked her soft, gentle, humble response. He saw in her mouldable soft material, ready to be shaped to his liking. He liked taking over people, moulding them, making them into 'something' and most of all he liked, no loved, their gratitude. That that gratitude might not come, or might carry resentment with it never occurred to him.

"That's very kind of you, but…"

"No buts, that's it then". He started scribbling down his address. A sudden thought occurred to Mira and her heart was filled with concern. Was there some other reason he was showing her attention? She felt a cold shiver run through her body.

When he finished jotting down his address, he looked up. He must have seen some of the concern on her face, for he added "My wife's not the best cook in the world, but you won't go hungry" At this she breathed. He did not live alone. He was married. No need for concern after all.

"Thank you" she said.

"At seven okay for you?" he added.

"Great, I'll bring some wine"

"Don't bother. I'm a bit of a connoisseur myself. Have a whole cellar of brilliant wines. I'll open your eyes to what real wine tastes like"

"Of course you will", thought Mira, but only smiled in reply. After he left, she wondered at the odd world she was finding herself in. Lost in thought she went over the conversation she had just had and the man she had met. What an interesting character. She smiled "here I am, in my own, supposedly 'real' world and it turns out Pixie was right, it feels no more real than the other places I have visited. His world is not the same as mine. It turns out I can see all kinds of different worlds without any flashes of light or angels transporting me elsewhere after all."

She remembered words from the Gita. How the world has no objective existence, not in the way we see and experience it. We all see and feel and experience the world through our own coloured personas. We see the world as we are, not as it is. What she saw and the world she lived in was so different from that of the publisher's. She could learn just as much right here from people that had been around her all along, as she could from all the magic wanderings possible.

She started to look forward to the dinner and seeing this man in his own setting, his home, with his wife, maybe children. She muttered a thank you, feeling grateful for this vision and this gift of insight.

Saturday came round quickly. She was writing again, this time with no expectation of being published. She was writing because that was what she did, without a need for a reason, simply because she enjoyed the process. It was part of her being, an essential part of who she was. It was a meditation in action of sorts. She could feel her soul open and clear as she wrote. She understood events, people and herself better as she described them. And she enjoyed the process immensely. It was her little gateway into a place that was deeper and more open, that offered infinite possibilities and beautiful gems.

She was greeted at the door by the publisher. Although he was staying at home, he was dressed well, perhaps slightly more casually than when they had first met, but rather smart for a home gathering nonetheless. He smiled at her and was once again a little too overbearing as he ushered her in with a "welcome, welcome"

His wife came out of the kitchen, wearing a colourful dress, her hair tied up away from her face. She looked more like an employee than a wife.

144

"Sorry, I look a mess" she said. "I'm running a bit late. I'm Anna. Make yourself at home. I'll join you shortly". She gave her hand a hurried shake and rustled off back into the kitchen.

There were no signs around of children. The house was quiet and way too tidy for there to be kids running around.

She was guided over to a seat; thick, soft cushions lay on it and Mira sank down as soon as she lowered herself into it. She felt lost in the huge seat, under the gaze of this overbearing man. He busied himself fetching drinks, talking about the weather, mentioning something he'd heard on the news. A constant background of words. Mira was not focusing on them. She was looking around her, wondering at all the objects the couple had amassed. The room was full of paintings, ceramic vases, glass objects, wooden carvings. "There must be hundreds of pieces here", she thought. The sheer number of the objects and the softness of her seat added to the overwhelming atmosphere in the room. They all fit in with each other, but she did not fit in there at all. Overbearing man, vast number of objects, a seat too large and soft. She felt she was drowning.

He noticed her looking around and smiled "I have the largest, and best I might add, collection in this city" he said with pride. Mira wondered why that mattered. The house was so full, she could barely breathe, there was no space. Why did it matter to him so much to have the largest or the best collection. Who decided what the best collection was, on what basis? Who cared? Collection of what? It was a load of 'stuff'. There was no coherence to the collection as far as she could tell. A thick, mad barricade of stuff, protecting the inhabitants from emptiness and space. Who cared really? Obviously he did. It added to his self-importance somehow, his desire to be the leading person in some field or another. Perhaps to have more made him feel bigger, better, more important.

"But they're just useless objects" Mira's thoughts rebelled. "They're not even nice to look at", but this thought she had to take back. Some of the objects were very intricate and beautiful. It was simply that there were too many of them to be able to really enjoy any one.

She pushed the thoughts away. How he lived his life, what was important to him, these were his business, not hers. Just as she wanted him to respect her book, which was what she felt was most important, what really mattered to her, so should she accept and respect what he cared about.

"Have you travelled much?" she asked, wondering if some of the objects had been collected on travels. Most did not look like they had been purchased locally.

"No, no, no" he said, gesturing as if brushing such a silly thought away. "I don't have the time. My work keeps me very busy. But this is my hobby. I order them from all over the world. After due research of course. You are looking at some of the best works ever made in this one room" He was so proud of his collection. She got up to look more closely at his things. She was curious, but also she wanted to give them something to talk about, something that obviously interested him. And last but not least, she wanted to get out of the swamp of a chair, where she felt too low, small and smothered.

The conversation became easier gradually. He was keen to point out details of what he exhibited and explain where they had come from. He was certainly in his element when talking about himself and his belongings. Mira started to feel easier in his presence in return. She could relate to passion and why not have that for a collection? He was much easier to get on with when talking about his collection, much more natural, more human, flesh and blood and feeling, rather than the cold, made up, fake composite she had first met.

His wife appeared carrying a tray of starters. She had also cleaned herself up and let her hair loose. Mira noticed how attractive she was, now that she had finished in the hot kitchen and smartened herself up. She now looked like a woman about to entertain, not one that is sweating away working.

Conversation flowed easily after that. They were a talkative couple and Mira became increasingly comfortable as the evening continued. She did not have to say much anyway. They talked as couples who have been together a long time do, finishing each other's sentences sometimes, but more often than not, talking right over each other. The conversation had turned to politics, the hot topic of the day. Mira hated politics. She could never understand why none of the politicians thought of ever using their power to benefit the people that had elected them as they should, rather than lying and spending every minute and every ounce of energy they had on backstabbing, breaking promises, lining their own pockets and preparing for the next election. They all pursued their own gains, power, wealth, often with aggression and with a strength, energy and determination they never showed towards the work they were being paid to undertake. The couple had different views however and seemed to hold one of the up and coming politicians in high regard.

"He makes sense to me" Anna was saying. "He will sort the economy out given a chance. Our prime minister's too useless and needs to go. I don't understand why she won't do the right thing and step down"

"Same reason as all of the others", Mira thought, "she wants to hold on to power for as long as she can, no matter at what cost, that's why". She disliked the man Anna was referring to. He had no steady opinions. He blew with the wind, shifting his statements depending on popular opinion. There was nothing trustworthy about him.

Her not-to-be-publisher added "sad state of affairs"

Anna was a far better cook than her husband had admitted her to be and the food was delicious, but as with everything else in this house, there was too much of it. Anna didn't eat a lot and Mira struggled with her own plate. She was beginning to feel tired and wondered how much longer it was going to go on for. It occurred to her that perhaps all she was, was a convenient distraction for them, some light entertainment to add colour to their week. The thought did not bother her. They had certainly added colour to her week. So why not.

As she watched them perform, she picked up an underlying anxiety, a drive of energy that kept them moving and talking at fast speed, as if they were worried an interruption might result in them being taken over, not by each other, but by some restlessness ready to burst to the surface inside of them. They were not settled and Mira wondered if they ever were calm and quiet, everything at peace in this overloaded, ready to burst at the seams, home of theirs. She suddenly wanted to reach out to them, hold their hands and say "it's okay, you don't need to run, none of this matters, it's okay"

Once dinner was over, he ushered her back to the over-soft seats and offered her brandy, which she declined. She was ready to leave, but was too polite to make a move so quickly after dinner.

He brought the conversation back to her book, animated from the food and drink, his face glowing with a tinge of red, cheeks flushed, eyes shining, in a far better mood than he had been earlier. And yet his increased self-confidence made it harder for Mira to like him.

"A thriller, that's what you need" he was saying, but this time Mira spoke up.

"It's not really my style. I don't think I have it in me. What I wrote came from my heart. It's what I want to share"

"It won't sell" for him that was the be all and end all of it, but Mira had her opening.

"You never know. But does it really matter? It's…"

He cut into her sentence, shock written all over his face "Does it matter? What else does matter? Child, you're too naive. Why else do you want to publish? Don't tell me it's for the love of writing. Then write, why try to sell your books at all? Keep them at home in a box. Then you can say what does it matter. But if you're trying to sell, it means you're wanting to make money. I'm telling you this book won't sell. I'm telling you what will sell. Why not give up your silly stubbornness. It's too childish for someone like you. Listen to what I'm saying."

"But" but she had no words. How could she possibly explain what she felt to this man. His values, his priorities and his view of the world were so different from hers. He could neither see nor hear her.

"I wanted to take it out there" she said. "To share it, in my own way"

He shook his head.

She started to feel frustrated, a feeling of dislike for this man spreading in her once again. She caught herself short. Was it not her ego driven pride that was raising its head, throwing up dislike towards this man? Did he not hold the same Divine essence in his self as she did? "And you also have your judgements and opinions" she reminded herself, "different, not worse, nor better. See the Divine and let go of the outer layers. He has a good heart, you can feel he does".

She focused on her heart, trying to pick out the gentler, softer elements in the man's face, trying to connect to him through her heart. And to her surprise it worked. Her heart warmed and it no longer mattered that he could not see her, that he was so carried away with money and how to make it, he could find no space for anything else. It was not her path, but it was his, and his way could not harm her unless she let it. Her dislike faded away.

They moved on to lighter topics and soon, when there was a slight lull in the conversation Mira got up, thanking them both for a lovely evening, but making it clear she was tired and it was time to go. They were resistant at first, whether from politeness or because they genuinely wanted her to stay longer Mira could not tell. But she managed to leave with a trail of further thanks and compliments.

He told her he'd be in touch. He said he was keen to know how her work on the thriller progressed. Mira was amazed at his insistence. Had he really not understood that a thriller from her was not on the way, now nor ever. She smiled, and it was genuine, and made her escape.

"We have to realise we cannot fight darkness with darkness"
Deepak Chopra

She was making an effort to listen to the news. She wanted to be aware of what was going on and not hide from the nastiness of the world, but the news depressed her so much, she could only take in a little at a time. At times like these she really wasn't sure what she could possibly do in a world like this. What use was any help she hoped to give, any effect she hoped to have. People didn't make sense to her. How could they do some of the things they did. Stealing when starving she could understand, but as far as she could tell a lot of the worst crimes were done when there was no obvious need and in broad daylight with everyone to see. They were somehow legal. How did politicians bare to look at themselves in the mirror each morning? How could they sleep at night? What almighty force managed to quell their conscience and any shred of humanity and compassion they might have been born with?

But it wasn't just the politicians. She could not understand the people who voted for them either. Could they really be that stupid? And it went further. There were the journalists, with their lies and sensationalism, their corruption and made up stories. And some businessmen too. Even care workers and people managing charities, on the outside working selflessly for the good of others, but on the inside cheating and lying. Corruption, lying, stealing were spread throughout the world, at all levels, in all different walks of life. Greed for wealth and power consumed these people and Mira could not imagine how it could all change and what any one person, or a thousand people could do to change it. And worst of all was that she saw no desire in people to change things. She thought of the world she had seen where the people had eventually perished, much at their own hands.

150

The parallels with where she was now made her shiver all the way down into her spine.

She felt desolate as she sat at her table staring into space. What could she do? Nothing came to her, no answer, no hope.

"Oh Pixie", she thought, "it's all very well wanting to help, but I can barely help myself, what chance do I have in this vast, corrupt world?"

Pixie was before her, twinkling bright as ever. "Maybe that's where you should start" she said "start with yourself and the people immediately around you. A beacon of light shines bright, no matter how dark the surroundings. In fact light shines brighter in the dark. Live your life the best way you can and be of help whenever you can. There is no act of kindness and compassion that is too small."

Mira's dark mood did not lift.

"Not a huge help, all things considered" she mumbled.

"You can't help everyone, Mira, but consider the one or two that you do manage to help. You might be able to change things for them, just enough maybe so that the virtues of those around you grow, and that light can then spread even if in just a small part of the world. You have to start somewhere. And all it takes is a few shining beacons to gradually light up the whole space."

After a pause she added "stay true to your practise. Inner strength and answers to your questions will come from that."

Lacking any better ideas Mira nodded. She settled in for her morning meditation. At that moment, it was the best, perhaps only thing she could do.

It took longer that morning to reach even a low level of peace, calm and concentration, but she persevered and reached some point of concentration at last. She found calm and peace inside herself and as she focused, her heart opened up to a vast source of energy. She felt that everything was okay really, beneath all the turmoil of the world, beneath the suffering, greed and deceit, calm seas prevailed. She surrendered to that immense power, the source. Her heart eased, her breath became subtle, barely there, the energy in her spine flowed. Nothing else mattered. After all, did she not believe that everything that happened to her was a gift from God? And was God not there, always, beside her, helping and guiding her? Did it not make sense that that was the case for the world at large? Maybe this was all happening for a reason. Wisdom comes through suffering. Maybe the world needed this to be able to move on to the next level.

When she got up, she had an idea. Not much maybe, but it was a start. She got ready to leave. "Start somewhere", she was thinking." Just see what might open up to you as you move on. Stay open."

She made her way through the streets to a homeless shelter she knew of. It was a cloudy, heavy day. The sun was hidden behind layers of grey. She walked into a charity shop that was part of the shelter and waited in line until it was her turn to be served by the lively woman working there.

She had come in here many times before. They had a large collection of books and music and she rarely left empty handed. The woman working behind the till had captured her attention from the very start. She was always lively, always smiling. She wore bright clothes, the mish mash of colours surrounding her body usually did not match and her whole appearance was a clash of bright purples, pinks, blues, greens and oranges, all bright and vibrant, clamouring against each other, fighting for attention, dazzling the eye. The woman welcomed everyone that entered the shop and her smile made Mira smile no matter what was going on in her mind at the time.

When it was her turn she asked about the shelter "I'd like to volunteer. How can I go about it?"

The woman sounded overjoyed at this and told her who she needed to contact and wrote her email address down, handing it over to Mira. As soon as Mira thanked her, she moved on to the next customer.

Mira went home and sent a short email to the contact person, Sarah. She felt better having taken a concrete step in a direction. She wondered how selfless her effort was. "I feel better myself, so am I aiming to help them, or myself?", she wondered. But Pixie's reply was already appearing in her head "That's the beauty of it. When we help others, we feel better ourselves, and we help ourselves in the long run too. It's a win win situation. It's not a sin to feel good. In fact the scriptures and holy people all agree that positivity, optimism, joy are our natural states and ones we should always strive towards. While depression, doubt are not worthy of us, states we need to try to avoid in order to progress on the spiritual path. Truly good actions make us happy, while selfishly striving for exclusively our own benefit, even if to the detriment of others, never does, even when we think it will."

Mira continued with her practise and also continued to write, although no longer with any thought of publishing what she created. Days flowed into weeks. She had not received a reply from Sarah, so she returned to the shop. The woman there was wearing an odd combination of yellow and green that day and looked as vibrant as ever. She was surprised Mira had not received a reply and said maybe Sarah was too busy. This time she gave Mira Sarah's phone number.

Mira made the call as soon as she got home. Sarah was not welcoming. She made it sound like she was doing Mira a favour by simply speaking to her and she said she'd send her some forms. Mira was surprised to be treated that way. After all, she was calling to offer her time and energy to their cause. Why the animosity?

The promised forms did not come, however, and rather than pursue it, Mira decided they could not need help very much if they were so indifferent about her offer. She gave up at first, deciding that maybe this course of action was not for her. But the thought persisted, so she decided to try somewhere else.

"Even giving for free seems to take effort in this world" she thought. "How odd."

Her next attempt was far more successful and she was signed up to teach yoga and meditation once a week at an addiction centre.

153

She did feel appreciated there, by the staff and the participants, and she enjoyed teaching them, but it was also quite draining on her energy and she found she was very tired after each session she taught there. Her heart went out to the people she met. Their souls were covered in a veil of depression, driven by their addictions towards continuously harming themselves, trying to find a way out, and yet not always succeeding. She wished some light could touch them and help them see. Her heart ached as she watched their pain.

Pixie, as always, was far more philosophical about it. "We each tread our own paths" she said. "We cannot always see the bigger picture, but trust that there is one. That path is one they need to go down and there is value in it for them. They need to find their own way. All you can do is be there, help in your way as best you can, but you cannot walk their path for them, neither can you carry them across. Part of what you need to learn is to accept things as they are and not get dragged down into darkness every time you see someone suffer"

"I don't know how to. Not when I see it right in front of me, all around me"

"There is wisdom behind it all Mira. There is always a point, a reason. Have faith."

"The world seems like such a dark place sometimes."

"And can you relieve darkness with darkness?"

Mira shook her head.

"The only thing that scatters darkness is light. And light does not do this by fighting the dark, or pushing it away with force. It simply enters the dark space and shines. And its light spreads. Think of those who have touched your life, with wisdom, or just a smile or a kind word. You can't do what is beyond your power to do and expecting miracles from yourself is not only unkind, it is also ignorant and abusive."

Mira sighed. It's not as if she could snap her fingers and change the way she felt.

"No" Pixie replied to her thoughts. "You can't. But understanding does change things. And forgiveness for your shortcomings needs to come from you. And have trust and faith. Where's your compassion towards yourself?"

"Can I not go away again? Just for a break?" her voice was practically pleading.

"You can, but can you not see that what makes being here harder and heavier for you is that you take it too seriously? When you go away, you think of where you are as an imaginary world, a stage which you can watch, or join the actors if you like and leave whenever you chose to. So you can be lighter there, more objective, more open. This world is no different Mira. Just as you separate your Self and watch what is happening in your body and your mind when you meditate, so can you separate yourself from what is happening around you and watch. Not with indifference, but some space, so that you don't drown in the story. It is all a veil, remember. What is unchanging and real is beyond this veil, beyond this drama."

"But it feels so real. For them it is real. For me it is real, even though I believe what you say in my mind"

"If it weren't, you wouldn't need to be here. It is your practise that will help you see. In the mean time, keep it in mind and try to extend your meditation into every moment of your life. Feeling desperate is going to help no one"

Mira felt exasperated. All very well to talk the talk, but to live it? But then she remembered to try to extend her forgiveness and compassion towards herself and her feelings eased off a little.

"You are constantly trying to find some great meaning to what you do. It's your ego Mira that demands you 'achieve' something concrete. It's your ego that wants to feel important in what you do with your life. But who says you should? Is it really more worthy and valuable to have wide, visible ripples as a result of your actions? Does the meaning a person's life have grow with their wider appeal and reach? What makes you think so? Who's path are you trying to walk? Don't you trust that you are exactly where you need to be right now, doing exactly what you need to be doing and that your duty is to do it as best you can with contentment? What makes you think you should be doing bigger things? And what makes you think such things would be better?"

"Yes, my ego" was Mira's sad reply. A fleeting thought of 'what's wrong with me' passed through her, but she would not allow herself to follow that thought. "Each moment" she said, connecting back to her days in the ashram, "each duty, each action, each thought, each result, make it all, no matter how small or insignificant, an offering to God". She smiled and looked up at Pixie "I will try"

That night, as she thought back over her day, things became clearer. Yes, she was demanding and it was her ego that was demanding. It demanded value, purpose, a sense of achievement. Whatever it was that was driving her, she surrendered it. She was determined to live in each moment, and do whatever she was doing as well as she could, without needing a reason, a result, a return, a sense of accomplishment. "At least", she thought once more, "I will try". And that was good enough...

We create heaven or hell with our thoughts. This world already holds heaven and all its possibilities within it. Spend some time in nature. There it is impossible not to feel absolute awe for this world we live in. If you allow yourself to, you will know that you are already in heaven.

"I am ever present to those who have realised me in every creature. Seeing all life as my manifestation, they are never separated from me." Krishna to Arjuna in the Bhagavad Gita, VI:30, translation by Eknath Easwaran

"There's more I'd like you to see" Pixie said one morning.

"Another journey?" Mira looked up hopefully. She could do with a trip somewhere. Her days had been blending into each other creating a kind of mist around her, with nothing to differentiate one from the other, nothing to make one special or interesting. And her energy and hope was losing colour in the mist, blending into the surrounding grey. A diversion would be welcome. Something, anything to re-kindle her interest in and passion for life.

"Yes. It's the same world mind, we're not going to a different one, just a different part of it. You'll feel like you're in a different world though. I think it will help you to experience how even on this same world, people create their own worlds very different from yours."

Mira nodded. She had already noticed that. Even in this very city she lived and grew grey in, surrounded by the same things and people as she was, she had realised people lived in very different worlds. Not just different internal worlds, the internal reflected on the external and they actually saw the outside world differently, responded to it in a variety of ways, ways she did not always find easy to understand. "We each see the world as our minds are" she said. She remembered more from her ashram learnings: "We look out through tainted glasses. Glasses that are all tinted by our characters, habits, upbringing, life choices, genes. All unique, but none clear."

"That's right. You live in a world that is coloured by your thoughts, feelings, attitudes. You create your lives through your thoughts. The Buddha said that well. As are your thoughts, so are you and so are your surroundings. Not only do you see through those glasses, but you also create what you see using them. In fact, this brings me back to what I have told you many times before, this world is no more or less real than the ones you have visited with my help."

"I'm glad I get to go somewhere else though" Mira said and closed her eyes. She understood what Pixie was telling her. She knew all that. But for some reason she couldn't live it. Her mind heard and kicked the notion away. Her body gripped to her habitual understanding of the world and refused to budge. Her habits, thought processes, assumptions, judgements were too strong. "Let's see what comes next" she thought and waited.

When she opened her eyes, she was sitting on a beach. Trees surrounded her, vast towering trees, some branches sweeping all the way down into the water. She looked up. She could see almond trees and coconut trees and large pines and many others that she did not recognise. The sand was black and wet. Fallen branches lay scattered around on the beach. Not thin, small branches, but massive logs, some the sizes of large trees. Stumps of trees, long broken off littered the beach. A huge log lay in the water tumbling in and out of the shore with the tide.

The waves smashed in one after the other, a huge yawning as a wave leapt high up into the air, lingered for a moment and then came crushing down, the foam roaring mightily as it met the ocean surface. The fierce strength of the ocean caught her breath. She watched the motion mesmerised. The sound the waves made dwarfed any other sound around her. The dark cave the wave created at its peak belied physical laws.

As each wave lifted its mighty mass, she thought of a snake lifting its head up ready to dart and bite, darkness showing in its open jaw, the lifted depths of the wave. She watched as the massive log rolled in and out. It astonished her. She couldn't even imagine how strong the undercurrent was if it could move such a large log in and out as it did.

It was early morning and the beach was deserted, except for birds twittering about and ants, she noticed, hundreds of them scurrying in straight lines, in a hurry to get their work done. But why rush? Their work would never be done. They efficiently and quickly worked from the beginning of their lives until the end, never resting, always on the move and always in a hurry. What a life. A wonder they never stopped to question the point, why?

Her eyes caught those of a monkey sitting in a tree branch close by. He was black all over except for his face and chest. Big black eyes were staring straight at her, unblinking. She gazed back out to the ocean. "I could stay here forever", she thought. And yet she had only been there a few minutes. It occurred to her that as with every place and every thing else, she would get restless and bored and be driven away by her need to move on.

In spite of its unfathomable might and roar, Mira was drawn towards the ocean. She found herself hesitating only slightly. She started to walk into the water. It was refreshingly cold. She closed her eyes, enjoying the soothing feeling around her ankles. Each wave brought the salty water up above her knees and then withdrew again, pulling the sand out from underneath her feet. She had no proper grip into the ground. Nothing that could save her from being lifted up by a large wave and carried right out into the ocean. The thought did not bother her.

She felt the sun hit her shoulders. It had appeared in the horizon and was reaching out to her through branches laden heavy with great green leaves and clusters of large fruits.

She wandered back out of the reach of the ocean and sat down again, allowing her mind to absorb the silence permeating out within the roaring sound.

The sun was already quite high up in the sky when she felt the desire to move again. She could see the odd person here and there on the beach. There was no one in the water though. She wondered how dangerous it might be, but the draw of the ocean was too strong for her to ignore. She took off her clothes and slowly entered the water. First she walked in until the water reached her ankles, or so she thought. The incoming wave splashed water all the way up beyond her knees. She walked in further and large waves threw water all the way up into her face. She did not withdraw. She allowed her whole body to gently release into the ocean, sinking quietly, under waves, under water, under and away from the reach of any noise. The world became muted, utterly quiet. A switch flicked and her heart was calm. Her mind was at peace and completely empty. A depth of quiet that was wrapped up in an embrace, soft, cool, infinite.

"Heaven", she was thinking just as a wave crashed right over head, drawing her down to the ocean floor with force. As she tried to pull herself up in vain, the wave surfaced bringing her up with it and throwing her back out again towards the shore. She came up spluttering and gasping for air. Before she could recover her breath and spit out the water she had swallowed, the next wave came crushing in. Then another one. She started to swim back. To her utter surprise after only a few strokes with her arms her knee hit the ground. She stood up and fought her way back out of struggle and lack of air onto the black, wet sand.

She threw herself down, out of reach of the waves, legs and arms spread, still struggling to recover her breath. She lay staring up into the trees, shaded from the heat of the sun, her breathing was still coming out in starts, the roar of the ocean saturating the air around her.

She felt like the cells in her body were moving with the waves. She closed her eyes, listening to the waves inside her body. She felt like she was a part of that vast body of water. And suddenly, out of nowhere, another sound caught her attention. It drifted in on the wind and then was gone again. She wondered if she'd imagined it.

She lay there with an overwhelming sense of peace spreading through her for a long time, the ocean and its waves moving within her in time to those dancing without. She had no desire to get up, but eventually her curiosity created enough strength and restlessness within her to force her to move.

She walked along the beach. Few people were out, and those that were looked like tourists. Their cameras at the ready, strolling, posing, laughing. Still the ocean reigned above them all. A bar/cafe appeared to her left, its shutters still down, a dark skinned man wiping tables and chairs as he set them upright in the sand. He was whistling a reggae tune softly. He was at ease. She saw no sign of life burdens on his shoulders or in his face. She envied him, his easy going attitude, his gentle calm and contagious ease and happiness.

"I wonder if I could be so content wiping tables, living in paradise". A part of her assured her she could. She would love to have that attitude and simple joy. She would love to lead a life without excessive burdens and stresses, without aims and 'what's the point's. Without the nagging questions: What's my duty, my role? But who was it that had created those burdens and placed them on her shoulders? It was she, herself. She would place them there wherever she went or get bored and search for burdens to create something external to focus on. That was her nature. Or was it? She was not sure, but something told her this man would keep his ease and unburdened calm in her city, while she would carry her burdens, doubts and worries here. What had made them like that? Why could she not relax and let go? What was the nature of her drive that forced her to keep going, on and on and on and on... She felt even more envious. She wanted what he had.

She saw a path winding up through the trees and decided to follow it. The path brought her up onto a gravel road, lined either side with low buildings, their roofs reaching far out over the structures that held them up on all four sides. Hammocks, simple wooden tables fitted around tree trunks and handfuls of plastic chairs were scattered under the protection of the wide, long roofs. None of them were showing much signs of life. The odd person here and there setting up maybe, but that was it. It was quiet. The loudest sound was still the roar of the waves. She kept on walking, looking around her, her heart at peace, her eyes feasting on the many colours greeting them. Dark reds, oranges, bright yellows, all shades of green imaginable. Every leaf, tree, flower or fruit was large and sturdy. A butterfly flew past her, such a bright blue she stopped in amazement, her eyes fixed on this glorious vision of nature and beauty.

She came across an open cafe. It was busier than the others she had passed. A few people were sitting around tables. A long wood table was set up at the back with stools propped up in front of it. There was the chatter of people and welcoming smells of cooking aromas wafting out from it. She patted her pockets, wondering if she would have the same luck with money this time and she found she did. She picked out a chair facing out towards the ocean, although the water was no longer in sight. She could still feel its presence. More of the tall, large trees that were everywhere were blocking her view, but even their dense growth could not shut out the mighty sound of the ocean.

A woman came up to her, an apron tied around her waist, pencil and notepad in hand. She had no idea what to ask for, nor in what language to speak. "Coffee?" she asked.

The woman nodded and walked off. Mira was hungry. She looked around for a menu, but saw none. Behind the bar though there was a black board that simply said 'Breakfast. Coffee. Fresh Juices.'

The woman took her time. When she reappeared with a cup of milky coffee Mira said "Breakfast?" The woman walked off again. "Obviously no need to specify what", Mira thought, wondering what would appear on her plate when it arrived.

She cupped the coffee in both hands. The cup was warm. She sipped. A sweet milky coffee, it tasted good to her at that moment, but then, anything would have.

She noticed a young man sitting at the bar, eating. He had a large board propped up beside him. A soft, dark green material was stretched over the board and off it hung a variety of necklaces, bracelets and earrings. Intricate designs made with copper, brass, white metal, different coloured stones. They were beautiful. A flaming sun caught her eye, with what looked like a large amber stone in the centre. And then she noticed the flute lying on the bar by his side. "So I didn't imagine it", she thought. That was the sound she had heard at the beach, mingling in with the waves, the ethereal, otherworldly sound, kind of magical, like Pixie Dust.

Her breakfast arrived. An omelette with a few bits of small ham in it and some kind of crusty, fried pastry on the side. The pastry was shaped as a circle and when Mira bit into it, she found it was empty on the inside and tasted of oil.

The food was too oily for her liking, but she ate what she could, her attention wandering from her plate, to the gravel road and then back to the man with the flute. He was in no hurry. He ate at a leisurely pace, a hint of a smile on his face. He had long black hair falling over his shoulders and was wearing nothing but a pair of long shorts. His eyes had a dreamy, far off look to them. She would have sworn he looked happy with not a care in the world.

She heard someone speak behind her. Spanish, she realised. It felt like being on holiday. She relaxed. Whatever it was she was meant to learn here would come to her and until it did, she would simply enjoy being there.

The young man eventually rose, gathered his things and left in the opposite direction Mira had come from. She did not follow. She had a feeling she would come across him again. This couldn't be a big place anyway, it had the feel of a small seaside village.

When the woman returned to collect her plate and cup, Mira paid. She leaned back in her chair, enjoying a gentle breeze brushing her face and the warmth that had pervaded the air with the rising of the sun. She could feel its fierce heat even through the shelter of the trees. Leaves rustled in branches and still the ocean roared.

Eventually she decided to make a move. She walked down the road in the direction the man had taken. The place had come alive while she had been eating. Little buildings were scattered either side of the road. Most of them were restaurants, with a few tiny shops scattered in between them. The path led her back to the ocean, where it flowed into an inlet. A river flowed out to meet it, waves flowing into the river and moving back out, leaving the trickle of fresh water beneath to continue its route down to join the sea. A small stone bridge crossed over the inlet and she saw an entrance on the opposite side. The sign informed her that this was the entrance to the national park. A little hut stood by the entrance. A man walked up to her and asked if she wanted a guide. She shook her head no.

She saw the man from the cafe seated on a stool just before the entrance to the bridge, his board of jewellery displayed beside him. Behind him was a cart without wheels, lines of coconuts with their tops chopped off sitting on it invitingly and a thin dark man standing behind, busy chopping a pineapple.

She sat down facing out towards the ocean, sheltered by a tree from the sun. She could hear someone beside her open metal shutters.

The waves roared and yet the water looked welcoming to her. She noticed a beach stretching out towards her right. White sand glittering in sunlight. Trees coming up all the way into the water, their branches lowering down to meet the ocean. She saw a red flag along the beach and then another one further up.

Her breath was calm. She closed her eyes and settled in for meditation. What better place to practise. She watched the energy in her spine flow up and down as the waves crashed in and out. A rainbow coloured ring of light appeared at her third eye and part of her focus settled on the light, darkness within and around it. Her mind went empty. Peace prevailed.

By the time she moved again, the little village had completely come to life. A relaxed pace prevailed, laughter ringing in the air, smell of fried food floating into her nostrils, people talking here and there, dog barks,… It was still serene and peaceful, but people were up and about, a gentle background noise of activity coming from the small buildings behind her.

She noticed the young man again, seated on a stool by his jewellery, his hands busy twisting wires into shape. She walked closer to him and sat on the ground watching what he was doing. He smiled.

"Welcome my friend. Please, you can try on" His English was clear, although his sentences broken, like a child's. And that matched his face. He held a childlike quality in his expression. One that had not endured or pained. One that was not bitter or resentful. One that was having fun, enjoying himself and simply floating. Were there any thoughts at all behind those eyes Mira wondered.

She touched the pieces hanging from his board, but hesitated to pick one up. He put aside what he was working on and picked up the bracelet her fingers had brushed. "Please. For wrist"

She stretched out her arm and he clicked the clasp in place. It had a red glow to it from the sun striking copper, a small amber stone in the centre, intricate patterns surrounding the stone spreading outwards like the rays of the sun. It was way too big for her.

"It's like the sun" she commented.

"Yes. Flower"

"Beautiful" she said pointing at his board.

"Yes. I am happy"

A broken conversation ensued. His English was not good, but he knew enough words to communicate and between her low level Spanish and his beginners English and the help of motions with their hands they got by.

He offered her coffee and they drank as she asked him about the different pieces he had on show. His prices were high

165

and she wondered who would pay so much for his jewellery, as beautiful as they were. He was asking for boutique city silver and gemstone prices, yet his jewellery was made of bits of wire and stone.

"A lot of tourists come here?" she asked.

"Yes, few. Not so much as" he listed off a few names. "More quiet here, but I like"

He picked up the piece he had been working on and Mira watched as the design grew out from a dense centre. He was quick with his fingers and she could feel his concentration.

The sun had grown in strength and she shifted her position to move back under shade. It burned what it touched. The man seemed carefree and light. The sounds in the background lifted Mira's heart, the waves, the music, people. But above all, always, the waves. The crashing of the ocean had not softened and all other sounds were dwarfed in comparison.

Mira leaned back on her arms as she enjoyed the warmth, the breeze and that indomitable, vast figure, the ocean. Not for the first time during her travels she thought "I could stay here forever". She had a yearning to swim, but when she looked out over the shore she could not see a single person in the water.

"Is it okay to swim?" she asked.

"Care, no" he replied. "Dangerous. Rifts and currents. Muy fuerte."

Still, Mira wanted to at least feel the water. She left his side and walked up to the ocean barefoot. A wave leapt up and soaked her nearly up to her hips and drew back leaving nothing but a trickle behind it. The water was pleasantly cool on her skin. She looked out to the ocean. Those huge waves, their continuous movement, they mesmerised her. She wanted to let go and become a part of it, flow in and out with the waves, become unconscious of everything but the ocean, lost in its rhythm.

She noticed a red flag a little further along the beach. "Too dangerous to swim" she thought, but how could she not?

She took a few more steps in and stopped. She bent her knees, allowing the next wave to wash right over her head. Bliss.

Refreshed, she walked back to the jeweller. It was too soon to break rules, but she knew she would eventually.

She asked him about his life and he was more than willing to talk. It seemed that although he lived here, most days he went into the neighbouring town, where it was busier. There were more tourists there. "I would not like that", thought Mira. The quiet was precisely what made this place heaven. It was funny to think that only a few minutes away there might be a busy tourist town. He sold his jewellery at a market there. He also played percussion drums with his best friend, who made silver jewellery. He had a girl friend somewhere, not here, not even in this country. She was visiting her family with their baby. She at first thought it was a short visit, but then through their conversation realised that what he called a visit was probably a move back home. She had been gone a year. Ever since their baby was born. But he was not bothered. For him she was on visiting leave and would return. He missed them, but he was happy and busy.

She found out that he had been living here for a year. It sounded like he had spent his life travelling around, making and selling jewellery, making friends, learning from other jewellers and moving on. She realised he must be much older than he looked.

He warned her about animals in the water and on the beach and repeated that she should take care. She wanted to return to the water. And he suggested she try further on down in the national park.

Mira took her leave, but she did not enter the park, instead she walked back to the water, pondering about the man's life.

The cool water contrasted sharply with the heat of the sun. As she waded in, she felt her limbs melt into the water. Her mind relaxed and she realised how much thinking it constantly did. The pause gave her the shock of a loud engine suddenly coming to a halt after you've become used to the sound of it, so much so that it is part of the background of your existence. And you don't even notice its existence any longer until it eventually stops. Now, in contrast, the few thoughts that passed through were scattered and light.

Waves crashed into her abdomen and chest. Some were so powerful they knocked the air right out of her, but she did not want to return to the shore just yet. She jumped up to meet oncoming waves and let herself drift with them after their mighty crash. Some roared towards her so strongly she had to jump and turn her back on them and hold her breath as she was pushed down to the ocean floor.

She returned back to the beach after a while and sat on the sand, watching the ocean. Her eyelids shut and her focus was naturally drawn back into her spine.

She had no idea how long she had been sitting there. When she eventually opened her eyes the sun was a hot ball and the shade had retreated away from her. The heat was overwhelming. She got up slowly, her limbs aching from keeping still in the same position for a long time. She went back into the water to cool her hot skin and let herself go under with the first big wave. Even in the water she could feel the sun's power. She knew she had to get out of its direct gaze. A few more dips and she felt ready. She waded out slowly towards the park entrance, the ocean had carried her quiet a distance away from the shore line.

She saw groups of people entering through the park gates, signing in at a makeshift reception, paying their donations. It was a small wooden structure, protected well from the rain, but too basic to be called a building.

The beach was dotted with a few people here and there, some wading into the water, some lying around on tree branches or beneath them. Some had brought folding deck chairs with them and sat quietly in those reading, or resting with eyes closed. Most were in groups, laughing, chatting, playing around. Small children were running into the waves and screaming. Some adults and children were lying on the sand, within reach of the water, constantly wet, the waves washing over them regularly. When a wave washed over them completely, head and all, they let out a happy scream, laughing. There were many people staying close to the beach, although waves reached above human height no matter how inland they were. They were so used to it, they looked comfortably at one with the sand and trees, and all were one with the ocean, governed by its moods, with no control over its power or movements, but happy to let it be the main player in their lives, letting it flow over them as it chose to. She followed the path through the trees out of the park.

The jeweller was still sitting where she had left him, although he had retreated slightly further back to stay in the shade. There were three of them now, laughing and talking amongst themselves. Passing tourists glanced at their wares, but no one stopped. The jewellers barely noticed them.

He called out to her as she approached them. "Join us for coffee friend" She smiled and nodded. He pointed to a tree stump next to them and she took a seat, her wet clothes cooling her skin, water still dripping down from her hair. The sun was already drying her.

She smelt burning logs somewhere, the smoky sweet smelt wafting over towards her. And closer by someone was baking. She was not sure what it was, but it smelt like bread, with a sweet edge to it. A skinny guy with a limp was setting up a stand just next to them, chopping the tops off coconuts and arranging them in a row. He brought out a packet of straws. Then went to work chopping up a pineapple exactly as the previous man had done. He was still there, but neither showed any indication of discomfort by their proximity to each other, nor any sign of competition. He also had a few other, large and colourful, fruit with him that she could not have named.

The men she had joined were at ease, conversing from time to time, and always laughing. They did not seem to have a single care in the world. She accepted the cup offered her. The coffee was nice and strong with lots of milk and a large amount of cinnamon in it. It was tasty. "What a good idea", ran through her mind.

She cast her eyes over their work. The first one she had met, Miguel, displayed his jewellery on a board. Colourful stones woven into designs with copper, brass and tin. One of them was hanging rows of bead necklaces and bracelets. He noticed her look at them.

"Local seeds" he said. "They healing"

The third one worked with crystals and stones too, but he mainly had silver pieces.

They caught the sun, reflecting it back in different colours and shades, at times too dazzling to look at directly. There were a few drums propped up behind the stall.

"We play drums" one of them said, noticing her interest in them. Miguel added "bars, restaurants, markets, beach. People love it. Lots of dancing and singing. Everyone welcome. Everyone clap and sing. We make happy." She smiled. She could tell they were proud of what they did.

"You all live here?" she asked.

"Now, yes"

"Where are you from? Before?"

"Mexico" Miguel said.

"Me, Dominical" another one added. The third one did not reply.

Gradually she managed to find out more about them. They travelled around, playing their drums, selling their jewellery. If sales were good and they liked the place, they stayed on for a while. They had learned different techniques during their travels and met many people. They liked it here. Between this little town and one close by, where there were many many tourists, they had been staying on for over a year. Although recently they had taken a trip out across the country to the west coast, where it was very busy and crowded with tourists. They were happy, because it had been very good for business and they had managed to sell quite a few items. But they would not want to live there because of the crowds. They told her the birds, especially parrots, along that beach had been amazing. The brightest colours possible, every range of colour and sound. They described it as heaven. And Mira thought, "I'm already in heaven".

They were happy and excited as they talked, proud of their lives and their travels and who they were. Everyone was their friend by the sounds of it. Someone they had met a week ago and only seen twice and communicated with bits of broken English was already a lifelong friend. Everyone was nice, everyone happy, everything beautiful, tasty, good... People that only paused to exchange a few sentences as they looked at the jewellery became 'friends'. The world was full of friends and Mira had already been included in this group. She did not feel like an outsider. The chances were they would never see each other again, but what did it matter. Their way of living and seeing the world ensured them of a never ending influx of friends that could quickly replace those who had left.

Looking around her Mira could imagine that being the case in a place like this. Surrounded by so much, such extravagant natural beauty, an easy, calm pace to life, the roar of the ocean, smiling people all around, yes, she could see how everyone would be a 'friend', how life could feel easy and good and the world a safe place of peace and pleasure.

She asked them about a place to stay. They all made suggestions, so Mira specified what she hoped for to narrow the options down.

"Somewhere quiet and away from tourists" she said. After a short discussion between themselves Miguel got up and offered to take her somewhere quiet, not far but far enough.

"You can still hear the ocean" he said, "but it's not so loud you can't hear anything else"

She thanked him, took her leave from the others and set out.

"Not far" he said again as they turned inland. They followed a dirt and pebble track. They passed sign after sign advertising lodges, bed and breakfasts and hotels, some including wi-fi or hot showers or food. The signs were set up at entrances to little paths leading up through gardens to single storey buildings. As with all the other buildings she had seen so far, they all held sharply sloping roofs, the roofs continuing way beyond the walls of the structures offering shelter from rain and sun. She wondered why at least cafes and restaurants had not thought of this simple solution back where she lived. It rained often there and gatherings tended to be constrained to stay indoors. These roofs, plus a heater in the winter would make the streets, squares and parks so much more interesting and lively. It would bring the owners money too.

Tall trees were scattered everywhere, large colourful bushes, red plants, orange flowers. Another bright blue butterfly crossed their path and even that little being was bigger and more dazzling than any butterfly she had seen before. Broken and emptied, dried out coconut shells littered the path and its sides. A dog lazily walked up to them, sniffed around for a while and started walking along beside them, before meandering off to one side, having lost interest. The path certainly was quiet and thankfully also shaded from the sun. It was a beautiful, peaceful route. Mira loved it already.

Miguel took out a phone from his pocket. She had not expected to see that. But her surprise was silenced by her mind very quickly. Why wouldn't he have a phone. Living hand in hand with nature did not make these people backward or technology poor. He spoke to someone in Spanish and turned to her. "The house next to me is empty" he said.

They walked for maybe fifteen minutes and turned off the track. They passed a house on their right. He opened a gate that reached just beyond the gardens of the house and closed it behind them. A man walked up to them as they approached. The two spoke in Spanish and then the man motioned to her to follow.

"I leave you here back to beach. Come by later if you like". Mira thanked him and followed the man up to the entrance of a small hut. It was painted pink, although the paint had faded in the sun and the rain. The hut next door was painted a bright blue. He unlocked the pink door and held it open for her.

It was cool inside. The walls did not reach up to the roof. The roof was very high. There was a trellis between roof and walls, covered in mosquito net. Twenty four hour fresh air, without the nuisance of mosquitoes and insects. To the right of the entrance she saw a small kitchen and a wood high table separating kitchen from living space with two stools leaned up against it. The table ran from the wall to a tree trunk which supported it and continued up to support the roof.

In front of her to her right was a solid shiny wood dining table with a sheet of glass placed over it. Four chairs surrounded it. To her left the comfort of a sofa and two arm chairs beckoned her, with a low table between, once again it was wood with a glass placed over it. Straight ahead she could see the bathroom and two doors either side of it leading into simply but sufficiently furnished bedrooms. Both beds had mosquito nets hanging above them. Paintings of butterflies and iguanas hung on the walls, all brightly coloured.

The man looked at her. "Perfect" she said, with a thumbs up sign and broad smile. Once he left, she looked around the kitchen. Everything she needed was there; simple, basic and more than sufficient. Even a grater, coffee machine, bottle opener and jug had been provided. There was a sponge and washing up gel and coffee filter papers too.

She walked out onto the terrace, where a chair had been set out. She sat down and looked out beyond the nicely managed garden to a dense forest. The garden was divided into sections with brightly coloured plants, flowers and trees. A dense green carpet of grass covered it with a small path meandering down the centre to the gravel path she had arrived from. Tall trees and shrubs divided her little piece of land from that of her neighbours. It was quiet, secluded, heavenly.

It was true, in spite of the distance, they had walked at a good pace to get here from the sea, she could still hear the roar of the ocean in the background. "This must be the most incredible place I have ever seen", she thought to herself. Her heart was overwhelmed by all the beauty that reached her eyes, the depth and vibrancy of colour was beyond her ability to put into words. Her ears were filled with the ocean, insects, birds, monkeys, leaves rustling in the breeze... The tranquillity of the place was beyond anything she could have ever wished for. She murmured prayers of gratitude as she made herself comfortable. She had no intention of moving any time soon, maybe ever.

Each person holds their individual truth in their heart. Always follow your heart and dream, not someone else's.

"He who shirks action does not attain freedom; no one can gain perfection by abstaining from work. Indeed, there is no one who rests for even an instant; every creature is driven to action by his own nature." Krishna to Arjuna in the Bhagavad Gita III:4-5, translation by Eknath Easwaran

"Freedom means the power to act by soul guidance, not by the compulsions of desires and habits. Obeying the ego leads to bondage; obeying the soul brings liberation." Paramahansa Yogananda, Spiritual Diary

Days flowed one into the other. They took on their own comfortable rhythm. She spent them swimming, wandering, writing, meditating, practising yoga. Rain came down often, several times a day and on and off throughout the night. When it did, it was powerful and heavy, like waterfalls unloading their burden onto earth. Even animals went quiet during the downpours and all that could be heard were the pelting rain all around and the roaring ocean in the background. Often it rained all night, leaving its place for clear skies and hot sun during the day. The frequent downpours through the day were truly welcome, refreshing the earth, trees, plants and her skin, the skies emptying like an overflowing damn, its walls crashing down releasing a mass of water from the sky, drenching the earth and everything on it within seconds. They ended quickly, once more letting the sun take over. Clothes, chairs, the earth were dry so quickly, you would never have guessed it had rained minutes before.

Miguel, her new neighbour, greeted her every morning. Once he brought over a couple of incense sticks. Her host spoke no English, but came by to check all was good practically every day, usually bringing a coconut with its top chopped off, so that she could drink the juice. Once she had finished, he'd chop the coconut in half with a sword and motion to her to scoop the flesh out with a spoon. Although she invited him to, he never joined her as she ate.

The only way she could describe this place was as heaven on earth. Beyond heaven in fact, it was more beautiful, vibrant, alive and peaceful than any heaven she could have ever imagined for herself.

Just before dusk and dawn, before there was any outward sign of either of them approaching, a cacophony of roars rose up from the trees. At first Mira was frightened, but she got used to the sound and wondered what kind of animal could be making such a mighty noise. The roar was so loud and deep, she imagined animals the size of a bulls, or elephants.

She asked Miguel after them one day and he said "howler monkeys"

"Monkeys?" she asked, too shocked to believe him. "But they sound like giants"

He laughed heartily. "No, he made a motion with his hands, signifying a size no larger than his forearm. "Black monkeys, white chest and face. Small monkey. Big voice."

Howler was an apt description, but really a monkey? He led her over to the trees and peered up into them for a few minutes, then motioned her to follow his pointed finger. She looked up in the direction he was pointing. Sure enough, there was a black monkey squatting on a branch, both hands lifted to his mouth. He was completely still, frozen mid-action, holding something he had been eating in his little hands. Large curious eyes were fixed down on them, unflinching, unblinking.

"That's what makes that noise?" Mira still couldn't believe it. They were so small and yet their howls so vast. She shook her head, amazed. But she got used to that too, she got accustomed to their sound and welcomed their message that the sun was about to work its way either into visibility, or out of it. Next time she heard their howls she noticed the gentleness behind the deep loud cry. There was neither anguish, nor anger in it. There was nothing aggressive in the deep throaty howl. It could have never come from a lion. It was not a hunting cry, nor an aggressive one. It was a howl, a greeting, a greeting to the day or night to come, to the changing states of the world, to the interplay and fluctuation between light and dark. No fear came along with that sound for her any longer. In fact, their howls brought joy to her heart. "All about your perception. The world is as we colour it with our minds. Simple." she thought.

Miguel repeated his invitations for her to come by to their jewellery stand, or join them in some bar or on the beach for music in the evening every day. At first Mira was so deeply at peace where she was and so content with her daily relaxed routine, she did not want to interrupt it with the energy of people and their commotion, sounds, crowds, no matter how pleasant. These were not what she wanted to be a part of. The tranquillity was special. He was so kind towards her though, she eventually felt obliged to go, no longer able to refuse his regular, warm invitations and said she would join them that evening. He gave her instructions on how to find them and went off with his jewellery stand to sell what he could.

That day her host brought binoculars with him. He walked out into the garden and gazed up at the trees as Miguel had done. After a few minutes he beckoned to her and pointed high up into one of the tall trees bordering the forest. He handed over the binoculars.

At first she could not see anything other than trunk, branches and leaves. And even they were all blurred. She started adjusting the lens and aiming it more careful in the direction he was pointing. It took her a long time to pick out what he was trying to show her. Meanwhile her host was both laughing at her and getting impatient. Eventually she did see it. "Iguana" he was saying, still laughing. "Pequeno", small. What she saw was anything but small however. It looked like a very brightly coloured, shining crocodile. It was lying across a branch high up in the tree. Bright green, yellow, black, brown. And huge eyes. It was incredibly beautiful. Mira felt awe and a warm joy in her heart. How exquisite, and strong. A giant lizard, or massively thick snake. She had never seen anything like it. Thick zigzag thorns were protruding out of its body. It lay completely still.

She made her way down to the ocean that evening in the dark. The odd streetlamp lit small sections of the path, leaving the surroundings in ominous darkness. Shadows played tricks on her imagination. There were so many rustling noises and grunts, so much scurrying around in the trees and the undergrowth, her nerves drew tight. But having taken this path so many times before in daylight, she mumbled words of reassurance to herself and continued. Luckily the sky was clear and the moon and stars shone enough light on her path that she was not walking in pitch black. Her eyes got used to the dark quickly and she knew the way down well. Not that it would have been easy to go down a wrong path anyway.

She reached the small cluster of buildings and semi-paved main road, which was lined with shops, cafes, bars and restaurants eventually, having grown bolder with each step she took. There was more going on in the centre than she had expected. It was such a sleepy village during the day. Music drifted out of various bars and the sound of talking and laughter filled the otherwise peaceful night. She walked down the main street until she saw the sign she was looking for. It was near the place she had had her first breakfast many days ago. Walking into a noisy, crowded space did not appeal to her. She noticed the smell of burning logs coming from the beach. The bonfire was out of sight, hidden behind dense trees. She hesitated a moment, torn between the feeling of a promise that needed to be kept to and the appeal of the bonfire, ocean and dark night sky. It was not a difficult decision. She walked on, searching for a path to take her down to the ocean. She found it easily, there were a couple of cars parked at the entrance to the path. She followed the sounds and quite suddenly she walked out into open space.

The ocean was as fierce as ever. In fact in the moonlight the waves took an even mightier and otherworldly apparition. The foam of the waves shone back at the beach momentarily and stood out strongly in the darkness surrounding them. The ocean roar was so strong, at first that was all she heard. Her gaze was transfixed on the powerful image laid out in front of her. It captivated her, drew her heart out, an awe and joy so forceful and expansive, she thought her chest would burst. Gratitude and love opened up within her. She wanted to walk straight into the magical dream worlds the waves painted for her, knowing full well she could not survive. She started to move closer, but other sounds caught her attention and she turned her head towards them.

She saw the bonfire off to one side and picked her way through fallen branches and almond and coconut shells towards it. She saw her neighbour with his two friends, two of them playing drums, one with a flute hanging by his side. A few people were up, dancing, others seated around the fire, shawls wrapped around their shoulders. She noticed an open guitar case with the guitar propped up in it.

She joined the group, taking a seat in the semi circle, towards the outer fringes. She moved quietly, hoping not to be noticed. She felt like an outsider. Not part of their energy, and yet in some odd way, perhaps purely because they shared the same magical location, connected to them. Her neighbour waved at her and she waved back. The mixture of the crashing waves with their white jaws, the rhythm of the drums, the breeze in her hair and the dancing flames gradually mesmerised her. Her mind started drifting, not quite empty, but not following any particular thought either, floating lightly through ether.

She had not spoken a word since her arrival, yet her sense of connection to this little gathering grew in her heart, a sense of belonging, oneness with all gathered there, their breaths and heartbeats moving in unison. The waves and drums whipped up a joy in her heart that made her want to dance. She did not resist. She started to move to the beat of the drums, her limbs swaying, her muscles joining in, each cell in her body combining to pulsate and beat with the drums and flow with the waves. She let them. She felt light and free like the wind and the waves. Others were joining in too. Her arms swayed and opened, her hips moved with grace, her face lit up with a smile.

And then a heavenly tune picked up, the sound of the flute drifted through the air, smooth, gentle, enticing. She felt the music in her heart and closed her eyes, moving to the calmer tune of the beautiful instrument.

She had no idea how long they had been dancing for when the flute stopped and just as she opened her eyes the drums picked up their tempo gradually leading to a crescendo. She sat down and watched as some in the group of dancers picked up the speed of their movements to match the drums. They were laughing loudly, freely, these people that came from cities full of stress, competition, anger, frustration, for at least this moment had shed it all and they were dancing as though naked, their bright souls shining in the night. Mira's gratitude rose up to her throat. She was glad she had come.

"Whatever masks people stick onto their faces", Mira thought, "whatever they do or say, beneath it all beats the same rhythm of the universe in all of us. The same fluctuating waves. Beneath it all lies joy and love. Remember this", she told herself. "Remember this feeling of joy, love and connection. Beneath all the layers we are, every single one of us connected in spirit. We all search the way to this feeling and we all get lost most of the time. And yet, dormant as it may be, it lies there, beneath the surface, in every single beating heart".

The drummers stopped, sweat gliding down their skins, shining in the moonlight. Their eyes sparkling little gems. Gradually people started to drift away, back to the bars, or to their beds. Anyone left on the beach sat down. Faces turned to the fire, a satisfied quiet pervading the group. And the ocean still crashed, waves rising and falling. She could feel the pull and push of the ocean inside her body, even though she could no longer see the tide.

She focused on her heart, where she was most aware of the pulsating energy and stayed with it, in a gentle meditation, her senses not shut off to the outer world, but not really connected to it either. The outer world was nothing but an extension of the energy pulsating in her heart.

Gradually bits of conversation started to rise up within the group, all spoken quietly, as if everyone felt the energy connecting them all and was afraid to disturb it with a sound too loud.

More people started to leave, while some others settled further, lying down around the fire, their shawls and blankets drawn close over their bodies. She became aware of a chill in the air.

"Where to from here", she wondered. Then pushed the thought away. "Be in the moment, no point thinking about the future". It amazed her how quickly her mind rushed back in with thoughts, taking charge once again, busying itself in anything but the moment, where it was not needed and would have to be quiet, where it could be at peace, a peace it did not want and forced away with everything available to it. It was afraid of the quiet, it would fight for its power to the end. She took her attention back to her heart, away from the mundane, pointless thoughts her mind was throwing at her.

Her mind had not worked it out yet, and she had not allowed it to think, she wanted to feel. But she felt in her heart she understood why she was there and what the message was. For now, that was enough.

She did not wait for the end. She was tired and wanted to take the feelings she had into her sleep, without breaking them in conversation. She waved a goodbye to the drummers and left.

The next day when her neighbour greeted her she invited him over for coffee. Their conversation was broken, limited by their insufficient knowledge of each other's languages, but it was enough. Gradually she was able to build a better picture of his life and she found it interesting. He turned out to be much older than he looked, as she had already guessed and he had travelled a lot. In fact this was the first time in his life he had settled in any one location and actually lived in a building. He had passed most of his life living in a tent, moving from one place to another, from one country to the next.

Everything was beautiful to him and everyone a friend. Mira thought the world needed more of his attitude, yet at the same time she could not help feeling that something was missing. She could find no depth beneath the surface and for all his travelling, he did not seem to have really experienced people or feelings. Everything had been enjoyed and passed through, but had they been truly experienced? No worries weighed on him. He was light in his soul. Wasn't that a good thing? And yet the lack of depth, of opinions or hopes or aims?

She had realised that his girlfriend and their baby were away with her family, he always said on holiday, but as she delved deeper into his story, it sounded more like they had left for good. And even that did not weigh on him. He assumed they would return, once he figured out a way for her to work here, but he was not driven to do much about it. It was a passing thought, an idea that may or may not materialise. And didn't seem to really affect him. He did not care. Was he above caring? A different way of seeing and feelings things, beyond such petty details? Or did he lack the emotional depth to really care?

"Nothing bothers him", she thought. "Is that really a good thing?"

But then, were they all not unique? They lived the way their nature drove them to. Some weighed down by concerns and stresses, no matter how small and insignificant, mostly self-made. Others oblivious to all things that might burden others in their situation. In a perfect world perhaps they should all be like him. But the world was far from perfect and lacking drive, nothing would get done, nothing would change. Was there such a thing as a better or worse attitude? They were all different. They all felt and responded differently, driven by their nature. Who was to say his was the better way. Sure, it seemed he was eternally happy and carefree, but something in the way he looked and spoke, something in his energy told Mira otherwise. She felt that beneath the surface their was a deep sadness, something missing, a feeling he avoided confronting or befriending at all costs. Lying in darkness, never experienced. Was not Mira's strongest drive to know and to understand? She would have been driven to bring those feelings out of the dark, she would have had to face them. And who was to say that was bad? Harder, for sure, but worse or better?

Anyway, she could not change her own nature and her nature drove her to think and analyse. She needed to learn, investigate and understand. A little more of his attitude would not go amiss though. A bit more of a carefree, relaxed attitude would make her life a whole lot better and easier.

He was happy roaming and she knew that as much as the thought appealed to her, she needed to have a purpose and a home. She knew what her purpose was, she could touch it, but could not have put it in words. All she could do was follow her intuition and keep searching, keep walking and learning. A sense, an intuitive drive. She knew that as long as she followed what felt right, she would find her path. As long as she stayed connected to her heart.

When he left she settled into meditation, clearing her mind and trying to just be in the moment. Let whatever comes up rise to the surface, she thought.

"Where to now?" she wondered gently. She could stay here, she would like to, but it was not her path. Not now.

"It's okay", she told herself, "you don't need to know the answer, it will come".

Meditate! Get into your spine, connect to your heart, the rest flows from there naturally.

"Closing their eyes, steadying their breathing and focusing their attention on the centre of spiritual consciousness. The wise master their senses, mind and intellect through meditation. Self-realisation is their only goal. Freed from selfish desire, fear and anger, they live in freedom always." Krishna to Arjuna in the Bhagavad Gita V:27-28, translation by Eknath Easwaran

She gazed out to the sea, salty water dripping off her and cooling her skin. She was puzzling over Miguel. For all his exclamations of everything being beautiful and wonderful; his jewellery, their surroundings, the drumming and music, the people, for all his 'friend's, there was something about him that didn't quite sit right with Mira and she couldn't place her finger on it.

He seemed like a genuinely nice, warm, happy person. On the surface. But beneath that surface? His energy did not suggest joy, certainly not calm. He seemed to move in a perpetual mist of impatience and light anxiety.

Mira closed her eyes. She always assumed everyone was good, she naturally trusted people meant what they said. She often trusted their words over her instincts. But had her instincts not proved right time and time again?

"Why can't you trust your instincts? Why shouldn't you?" she asked herself. What were her instincts? That he was not as happy as he announced to the world. That beneath his carefully painted mask, he was restless? There was an emptiness to his energy, something lacking, no deep warmth or inner calm that suggested contentment. But why? He lived in paradise and did what he loved to do. Nothing tied him down, nothing held him back, he carried no excess weight of life pressure, worries, duties and responsibilities. He lived with nature, his body pulsed with the beat of drums, the might of the ocean, the warmth of the sun, his hands created. How could he not be at peace? Perhaps he was happy? Why did Mira have to question it?

But her mind would not settle. She felt back into his image. He could not be still, even for a moment. His activity was not one of excited energy, it did not speak of joy. It was restless, a relentless drive that would not allow him to be still or at ease.

She had watched him with tourists, "I create many beautiful things, please, try". It was not just an invitation, but a plea. He had to keep moving. Even when they shared a coffee together, conversing, he would sit for a moment, then jump up, finding something else to do.

She had noticed, he did not like being alone either. He always gathered people around him. But he did not sit with them, or get to know them. He gathered them and then kept moving around restlessly. He never asked her any questions about herself, or her life and only told her about his as replies to her many questions. His main conversation was repeated clichés about beautiful place, beautiful jewellery, happy and friends. And there was no questioning any of this, no thought about people or himself. No understanding of who they were, or who he was. It felt like he was constantly running. Running from what lay beneath, the emptiness never even peaked at.

She knew people who were generally happy and content. But theirs she could feel. It was contagious. It reached out to anyone that crossed their path. They shone from within with optimism, positivity, energy. It was uplifting just spending time with them. And yet she found being around Miguel draining. He sapped her energy. "No, this is not better either", she thought. "There is more to life. We cannot spend it running from ourselves".

She had liked his friend much more than Miguel, although he did not go on about how everything was beautiful and everyone his friend, but his energy was far more at ease.

Mira felt he was comfortable with his life, doing what he did, being who he was. She sensed no great driving restlessness beneath his smile. There was more awareness of himself and his surroundings that manifest as a sense of groundedness and presence within him.

It didn't matter really. Why did she feel this need to understand? What were these things to her? What business of hers? She knew the answer. It was because that was what she did. For better or worse, she always wanted, needed to know, to understand, to feel.

The same world as hers, and yet she could have been on a different planet. And at the same time it struck her how similar people were everywhere. They were all searching. Even an easy life in paradise would not shield a person from the yearning for something more. Some never questioned the yearning, they refused to acknowledge its existence. Some tried to fill it with worldly goods, with wealth, power, people, relationships. But it was there in all of them. An inability to find complete perfect peace and happiness, unbroken by outside events that were for the most part completely out of their control. There certainly was a peace and joy that lay in each and every human heart, yet it managed to stay so elusive. A deep contentment and joy that had shone for Mira in meditation sometimes, spreading out within her to take over all that she was, there for a moment, then gone with the rising of the next thought in her mind. But arriving faster and staying for longer each time she practised. That was the centre piece of her life, she realised, the building block from which all else would grow. The peace, joy, connectedness she received while in meditation.

And her path? To connect with others from that centre and share its source, however little her knowledge may be and however small and limited her reach, to share what she could, so that others could experience it too.

She made her way slowly back into the sea and let go as a wave crashed into her, knocking all breath out of her lungs for a moment. She went under, cold water, one with the wave, and then was thrown back out against the shore. She sat there dazed, catching her breath. No fear, just peace.

The sun had made its way half way up the sky. It blazed hot. She crawled under the shade of a tree. A bright yellow bird, tiny, flew down, caught something in its peak, flew up into a branch and ate its catch in two big gulps. Golden bright yellow body, orangey brown wings and a white face, streaked with a black line. Off it flew into the trees.

She did not want to return to the city. Connection was easier here where the energy of nature was stronger than all else and within her reach at all times. And just being here helped Mira connect to what lay beneath, in her heart, in her spine. But people need a sense of purpose in their lives and we all have our duty, our path, which we are driven to follow and we cannot find peace until we are set on the path of our calling. She knew staying here was not her life at this time, no matter how much she wished it was.

"Is there more?" she asked Pixie in her mind. Unnecessary question. There was always more, she knew that. As long as she had a body, there was more to learn, see and feel. More layers to peel off and free herself from. More baggage to unbuckle and throw off. More connection to find. More to let go of and more to find out. Gratitude swept through her, for the opportunities she had been given, the gifts that taught, and all those wonderful people and beings who supported and helped her.

She sat upright with eyes closed and drew her focus into her spine. She did not understand the way the world worked, not even the way she worked, but she knew that all she could do and in fact needed to do was to keep up her practise, nothing else mattered as much, everything else fell into place around her practise.

What is sadness, but a fleeting state, poignant and beautiful, if gazed at with love and let go of, without clinging on to it, trying to mould it into our very being?

"Mindfulness is the energy of being aware and awake to the present moment. It is the continuous practise of touching life deeply in every moment. To be mindful is to be truly alive and at one with those around us. Practising mindfulness does not require that we go anywhere different." Thich Nhat Hanh

"Pleasures conceived in the world of the senses have a beginning and an end and give birth to misery, Arjuna. The wise do not look for happiness in them. But those who overcome the impulses of lust and anger which arise in the body are made whole and live in joy. They find their joy, their rest, and their light within themselves. United with the Lord, they attain nirvana in Brahman." Krishna to Arjuna in the Bhagavad Gita, V:22-24, translation by Eknath Easwaran

When she finished Pixie was waiting for her, watching with her usual smile on her face.

"Is it time?" she asked.

Her answer was, rather annoyingly, another question "Do you feel ready?"

Why did Pixie force her to decide? Mira wanted to be told what to do.

"No. And yes. I want to delay, but I suppose now is as good a time as ever"

"You can delay if you like"

"Is there more Pixie? Is there more you want to show me?"

"Perhaps. But not right now. You stay or go back, your choice."

"Go back to what? I know I need to, but I don't want to, not just yet. In the struggle between a person and their environment, the environment always wins. That's what my teacher told me. The environment I return to is not one I want to be a part of me and I am not yet strong enough to keep it out and to keep this peace within me when I'm stuck there"

"Each time you return, you are stronger. And you are a part of that environment, and yet, you can make your environment whatever you want it to be. We mould our surroundings and our life through our thoughts. First comes the thought, then the physical appearance of it. We are what we think. We do as we are. It all starts with the thought."

"But here nature dominates. Here I can feel connection at all times, I'm reminded of it with each breath and sound. It is easier"

"How long do you think you could live here before you start to feel restless?"

"Here? I might not" she replied, but she wasn't so sure. "I felt more restless back there. I felt I ought to have a purpose, something solid to live my life around. I felt I owe it to the universe somehow, it has given me so much. But I don't feel that need here, I'm at peace."

She wondered if she could not keep this peace and sense of connection with her if she returned. Would she not remember it?

After Pixie left, she sat listening to the waves, her eyes closed, focusing on her heart. She would wait until an answer came, until she knew in her heart and not her mind. Doubts whirled around and she struggled to keep her focus. Her mind was jumping from thought to thought without settling, refusing to empty or to calm down. She felt incredibly alone suddenly. She so rarely felt alone, no matter where she was, the feeling took her by surprise. Alone and so tiny small and insignificant. She did not mind feeling insignificant, that did not jar with her, but the sense of isolation did. Who was she to help? With what knowledge or strength? This tiny little body, cast out into this harsh world. What could she really do? Who the hell did she think she was?

She forced her focus back to her heart, but her mind was too loud. And out of nowhere she remembered what would help her, always: faith. And the surest way to connect to faith that she knew of was prayer. She prayed. Her mind quietened, her heart warmed.

"I will know what to do" she thought. "I will know"

She let the days pass, let them continue to blend one into the other. She let herself drift, swimming when she wanted to, sleeping when she wanted to, reading, practising her yoga and meditation, letting herself be, without control or force.

The thought of returning daunted her at times. She wanted to be told what to do, by someone she could trust. It occurred to her that might be part of her lesson; that she had to find her own way and trust her own intuition. She needed to learn to trust her inner voice, trust that it would guide her well, that it would know the right course of action. She realised how little faith she really had in herself, how often she questioned her own instincts when others around her disagreed. And anyway, there was no such thing as a mistake. What we call mistakes are purely lessons that help us grow.

Eventually though she knew she had to return, even if just to test herself, but she knew it was more than a test. Pixie was right, she needed a sense of purpose, she could not drift for long, something inside her would not let her. And when she looked at Miguel, she wondered if it let any one of them. He was restless and his smile did not reach his eyes, but he fled from questioning it. She would not. She could not. She would face whatever she needed to.

"I'm ready Pixie" she thought and closed her eyes.

She felt Pixie's presence, but hesitated. "Will you stay with me?" she felt a sense of dread, as if this might be the last time she saw Pixie.

"I've always been with you Mira. You just forgot. It's up to you to connect with me, or to the world around you, or to your heart, or your faith. It's always up to you. It's up to you to believe or not, to be strong or not, to be lonely or not, to be depressed or happy. Always up to you. None of these things vanish or stop existing, or run away. It's you who loses connection and it's up to you keep it alive."

Mira felt slightly reassured, but her distrust towards herself was strong. She forced herself to open her eyes. And as always, she saw Pixie smiling. Always smiling.

"Are you always happy Pixie? You look like you are."

"I feel sad sometimes or concerned, but I don't become 'unhappy' by those feelings. Emotions are sensations, feelings that can be poignant and beautiful or interesting. How they make you feel is a matter of your attitude towards them. Endings can be sad. Or when I see people do things that I know will hurt them, I feel sad. I feel sad when you feel lost or depressed, for your suffering. But I know it is a part of life and what you feel is a part of your process. I also know it is not necessary for you to feel that way. None of this matters in the way you think it does Mira. People get so carried away with temporary things, so often insignificant things. They go down into the depths of depression for something that viewed a different way is a gift. They become their sadness, when it is only a passing emotion. They shut down and run from feeling, when feelings create such a rich mosaic of experience. But even those states are a part of the leaning curve. You try everything to reach what you think of as happiness and it's through that continuous trying that you finally realise how fleeting all these states are. You experience how it all comes and goes. You can't come out of ignorance without effort. Gradually, with effort, with shed tears and aching heart you learn. But the process also includes beauty, love and joy. Otherwise it would be too unbearable for anyone"

"There's one more place I'd like to show you" she added after a pause. "Close your eyes"

Mira obeyed.

The only way to get rid of darkness is to shine a light. And just like that darkness vanishes, leaving its place to bright light.

"One evening an old Cherokee told his grandson about a battle that goes on inside people. He said 'my son, the battle is between two wolves inside us all. One is Evil: It is anger, envy, jealousy, sorrow, regret. Greed, arrogance, self-pity, guilt, resentment, inferiority, lies, false pride, superiority and ego. The other is Good: It is joy, peace, love, hope, serenity, humility, kindness, benevolence, empathy, generosity, truth, compassion and faith.' The grandson asked, 'which wolf wins?' The old Cherokee simply replied, 'The one you feed'." Anonymous

"Your work is to discover your world and then with all your heart give yourself to it" The Buddha

When she opened her eyes she was at first too dazzled by a warm golden light to be able to pick out anything else, but gradually she began to see. All around her were many sparkling pixies. All of them were smiling, all looked busy, all happy. She watched them in their activity, as her vision became clearer. She noticed a golden thread, a connection stretching out from each one of them and like a dream, she saw their threads reach down to earth. They were all, each one, connected to individual beings on earth. People were darting around far below, in a hazy, dream like world. How grey and heavy they seemed in comparison to these bright, glowing angels. And every single one of them was connected to a pixie of their own. Every single person on earth had a direct link to magical entities. Ones that fulfilled wishes and dreams. Ones that could answer all perplexing questions.

She turned, awed and amazed, towards Pixie, who was watching her closely. "You are all connected" she said, "but most of you are too wrapped in your dream world to notice us.

You so believe your world is all there is, you can't see beyond it. You don't feel our gentle tugs at your hearts."

"How grey it is" Mira said. "How unreal it seems from here"

"And yet you make it your one reality. You choose to make it your whole world, Mira" Pixie pointed towards the grey heavy mass. "And yet all the while this is all within your reach", now gesturing to their immediate surroundings, so full of light and joy.

Mira watched the movement of her people. She felt sad for them, herself included. She felt a desire to help, to lift their heads up to the sky and see this glowing brightness, but the fog that surrounded them was impenetrable. "But why? And how?"

"As heavy and grey as the fog looks at times, it's up to each individual to reach out. Just a wish, a prayer, a glance up and you could all see through the dense air. We can't force it. But we can follow and stay close, waiting for each person to gaze up, to be open enough to feel our presence. We answer prayers and for a moment someone might feel us there with them, but they forget quickly. Humans are endowed with this incredible ability to forget and move on, otherwise life would become too unbearable but it comes with its price. You also forget God, pixies, love, sense of connection, of impermanence, of gratitude, of beauty."

"And there's more than this here as well, isn't there?"

"Yes, there is more"

Mira watched, taking it all in as best she could, with all her senses, especially her heart, wanting to register it all, and engrain it into her very being, into every cell of her body.

Then she saw more threads reaching up beyond them. She could not see where they led to. "And those?" she asked.

"They lead further, to higher dimensions of being. You will go beyond this as well when the time is right. You'll be able to rise up and see the larger pattern. And I expect we'll all one day rise up beyond that one too. But look down Mira.

Do you see how you trap yourselves in darkness? You pull that fog close in, afraid to let it go, believing it is what's real. Afraid of the unknown. Ironic that the unknown is so light and bright isn't it? You try to blend in with the fog, when you could break out of it. You make it your whole lives and restrict your breathing to match it."

"None of us want this"

"But you hold on to it, afraid to let go of what is familiar, afraid of what breaking through might mean"

"But why?"

At this Pixie shrugged. Mira was not sure she had an answer.

"How?"

The world she was looking at, her world, looked so grey and bland. Why did no one look up? They were so preoccupied. And yet it looked unreal too, blurred with fog and stuffy air. And yet so temporary.

Everything looked like she could glide her hand right through it, insubstantial and yet dense at the same time. All the people down there were like dense clouds, surrounded by lighter clouds and as her eyes adjusted, she started to recognise these clouds. They were their thoughts, feelings, inspirations, plans. All part of that fog-like mass. It was as if people were gripping on to their heavy thoughts and their troubled weight, surrounding themselves with it with all their strength, clinging to it as to life. It also looked like she could blow it all away and the fog would disperse.

"It wouldn't" Pixie said, reading her thoughts. "In fact it would be easier for you to blow a thousand year old tree away then those swirling thoughts and feelings they have gathered around them. Thoughts are strong, Mira. You know that. They have an energy, a mass of their own. That's why they're so hard to shrug off and keep away. That's how they mould themselves around individuals, clothing them, suffocating them in layers, fitted tightly around their souls."

194

And then Mira noticed little dots of light. Some so weak, she had to strain her eyes to see. And others, they were glowing. And where there was light, the surrounding fog was much lighter. The light pierced through and cleared out a path. "That's how things will change" Pixie said. "As more and more people find their inner light and feed it with their focus, faith and love, the fog around them will become weaker, dispersing gradually. Their light, the clarity around them affects those near them, and gradually, the light spreads. That's where humanity's hope lies"

"And that's my purpose" Mira mumbled. "No matter how small I might feel, the light has to spread from somewhere, it has to start somewhere. But it's so hard. Isn't it Pixie? It's hard to keep the light glowing. Look at all that fog. How can I keep it alive and not get drawn down into the dense fog?"

"You can. Follow your path. Keep your faith alive. Remember what you have seen. The light is always there, inside you. It's not about finding it, it's about letting it shine through, about not smothering it or crushing it down with heavy thoughts, fear or anger. Keep feeding all that is light, love, faith, compassion, forgiveness. Let your heart be your strongest guide. Remember, whatever you feed becomes stronger. Whatever feeling or thought you feed most, will dominate you."

"It doesn't matter what I do specifically", Mira mumbled, "what matters is how I do it".

She felt comforted. She could hold on to this. No matter how dark things might seem, the way was clear. Focus on the dark and it gathers round you with increasing strength. The fog will be there, but she need not focus on it. Over time, the light would melt it away. All she needed to do was focus on the light.

Her old room felt small and airless when she returned. It was a cold, grey day and city noises surrounded her. She glanced down at the papers piled on her desk, books scattered around everywhere. She sighed and started cleaning. Moment by moment, with her heart as her guide, she would tread her path towards the light.

"You have the right to work, but never to the fruit of work. You should never engage in action for the sake of reward, nor should you long for inaction. Perform work in the world, Arjuna, as a man established within himself – without selfish attachments, and alike in success and defeat. For yoga is perfect evenness of mind." Krishna to Arjuna in the Bhagavad Gita, II:47-48, translation by Eknath Easwaran

"Live each present moment completely and the future will take care of itself. Fully enjoy the wonder and beauty of each instant. Practise the presence of peace. The more you do that, the more you will feel the presence of that power in your life." Paramahansa Yogananda, Spiritual Diary